A Second Shot at Love

SAMANTHA MICHAELS

Thank you to my husband and our dog, my amazing friends and family, my fellow authors, my PA Zoe, and the rock stars who inspire me.

Chapter One

I t was 4:30 AM on the first warm Friday morning of the season. Alexandra Peterson, Alex for short, was awakened out of a dead sleep by the shrill beeping of her alarm clock, which Alex swore went off earlier and earlier each day. She sighed, knowing it was a small price to pay for owning one of the most successful farms in rural Lancaster, Pennsylvania. As the only child of Bryce Peterson, Alex inherited the farm when her father lost his battle with cancer.

Her farmhouse is a beautiful one-floor home, including a large bathroom, three bedrooms, a living room, dining room, kitchen and a small office. There's more than enough room for her and her beautiful Black Lab, Holly. What was missing was a man to share her life and her home with. Maybe someday, she thought. The living room fireplace featured a mantle on which her father's ashes and her favorite picture of him rested. As she stood and gazed at the urn, she started thinking back over her life, both what she remembered and what her father had told her.

Her mother Alana, born and raised in urban Los Angeles, was unable to handle the rural life and left them when Alex was only two. Alex was left with only the memories that her father had shared. Except when she was in school, Alex was always by his side. It never occurred to Alex that she missed out on anything not having a mom, especially having Margie in her life. George and Margie never had children, so to them, Alex was the daughter they never had.

From the time she entered kindergarten, Alex was that kid that everyone made fun of. She was shy and introverted, always unable to make friends. Add to that the fact that she was taller than all the other kids and didn't have a feminine bone in her body, she was a goner. Whenever parents would invite classmates for birthday parties, there was never an invitation with her name on it. Her only friends growing up were the animals that her father raised.

Instead, she immersed herself in her studies and ended up graduating at the top of her class, earning the distinction of Valedictorian as well as winning awards in both the math and business departments. As long as she lived, she would never forget the look of pride on her father's face as she delivered her speech at graduation. She saw him tear up when she spoke at length about the amazing and positive influence he had on her life. Alex could have had her pick of colleges but she wanted to stay and help her dad as he had recently been diagnosed with cancer.

On a personal level, things changed for Alex after high school. She started to come out of her shell and found a great group of girls that she became close friends with. She also discovered how much she enjoyed sex. There was a diner not far from her family's farm where all the dudes who were into rock hung out, so of course, that's where you could find her when she wasn't helping at the farm. Unlike the snobs at her high school, these guys definitely appreciated her and her curvy figure. She was never without someone to fuck.

Physically, she was definitely satisfied, but there was always something missing. She found herself longing for that relationship, but so far it eluded her. At least until one fateful night. One Friday night, she was feeling restless and lonely, she decided to go check out the new rock club that had opened in downtown Lancaster. An up-and-coming local band, The Hounds, were playing that night. Alex had seen them live a few other times, and damn their lead singer, Dean Fox, was one fine specimen. The club's owner was also her dad's lifelong best friend, Jake Matthews, or Uncle Jake to Alex, so the front-and-center VIP table was hers anytime she wanted it.

Dressed in her favorite low-cut AC/DC t-shirt and a pair of tight jeans, she headed to the club and sat down at her table. The Hounds started their set, and when Dean came on stage, Alex's heart nearly beat right out of her chest. Before her stood a six-foot, two-inch rock god. His long dark hair and crystal blue eyes were mesmerizing. That night, he had opted to have his shirt open. She couldn't stop staring at his sexy chest, with its light smattering of dark hair and a happy trail that she would love to run her finger down.

Her eyes kept shifting between his chest and that oh-so-hot bulge in his jeans while she experienced one eargasm after another listening to his beautiful voice. She was so into his lower half, that she never noticed that he didn't take his eyes off her the entire time he was on stage. The Hounds played for about an hour before exiting the stage to make way for the next band in that night's lineup. Shortly after their set, Uncle Jake stopped by her table and sat down.

"Did you enjoy that last band?"

"Hell yeah. And wow, that lead singer!!!"

"It appears you made an impression on him too."

"How so?"

"He asked me if I would bring you to his dressing room so he could meet you."

"Ummm...okay."

Alex followed Uncle Jake backstage to the dressing room area and knocked on the door. Dean opened the door in just his underwear and she almost passed out cold.

"Dean, I'd like to introduce Alexandra Peterson."

Dean smiled and for the second time, Alex almost went down.

"Nice to meet you," Dean said as he looked her up and down.

Unable to remember how to speak, Alex just nodded, which made Dean smile even bigger.

"Would you like to come in."

Again, all she could do was nod. Dean waved her inside and shut the door behind her.

"Have a seat and take a deep breath. I'm just a dude."

"You're sexy."

The second those words, escaped her lips, she turned a deep shade red, completely mortified.

His eyes on her ample breasts that were spilling out of her shirt, Dean said, "Not as sexy as you."

If possible, she turned an even brighter shade of red then took a deep breath in an attempt to calm her nerves. The deep breath made her chest heave and Dean's eyes went even wider. Damn, she is fuckin' hot, he thought to himself.

"So, why did you want to meet me?"

"Wow, you can speak after all. As to your question..."

Instead of telling her, Dean sat next to her, put his hand on the back of her head and pulled her in for a kiss. He eagerly jammed his tongue in her mouth, quickly igniting a fire between her thighs. She intertwined her tongue with his, moaning at how amazing his lips felt on hers. After several minutes, they finally came up for air.

"Damn, woman, that was hot. I wanna fuck you."

Now fully recovered and back to her usual self, Alex shocked him with her response.

"Oh fuck yeah. Get that dick inside me now."

Dean removed his underwear and sat on the couch, just staring at her. She stood up and did a slow, sexy strip tease for him. Now completely naked, she sat in his lap, straddling him until the full length of his huge dick was inside her. She rode him hard and fast until they both exploded, screaming in ecstasy. She stayed on his lap, gazing into his gorgeous eyes.

"Fuckin' hot, woman."

"Mmm, so damn good."

Alex climbed off his lap and sat down next to him. She couldn't believe how amazing he felt and she hoped she would get the chance to fuck him again. Instead of waiting to see if that chance might come, she took her hand and put it between his sexy thighs, stroking his cock. She felt him quickly get hard again.

"Oh fuck."

"I want you. Fuck my pussy hard.

He stood, facing her and spread her legs wide. She felt his dick fucking her hard and fast, his balls slapping against her ass. She was screaming in ecstasy as he pounded her like no man had before. He filled her with another huge load of hot cream as her body quivered with an intense orgasm. He sat down next to her, their chests heaving after their intense fucking.

"I'm starving after my performance. Would you like to grab something to eat?"

"Which performance?"

"Naughty girl."

Alex smiled as they both get dressed and headed to a diner near the club to enjoy some coffee and breakfast. They sat and talked for hours, enjoying getting to know each other. When they were done they walked outside to their cars to head home.

"Alex, I had fun tonight. Can I see you again?"

"I would love to."

"Dinner tomorrow night, actually tonight since it's already morning?"

"Yes."

They exchanged phone numbers and addresses and firmed up their plans for dinner. Dean hugged and kissed her, causing her insides to completely melt. No man had ever affected her like this. Dinner was so much fun, so they made plans to see each other again. They continued dating and before long, they had fallen in love. Alex felt like she had found the one. And holy shit, was the sex incredible.

During the week, she handled things on the farm, but spent her weekends traveling to gigs with him. She loved hanging out with the band and she especially loved watching her man perform on stage. He always looked so damn sexy and his voice was incredible. Performing always got him amped up, which was good for her. He loved to burn off that extra energy with her, so she got to spend a lot of time naked in his arms. She lost count of how many dressing rooms she'd gotten fucked in.

Things were going wonderful until Dean got news that changed the course of their lives. They had just finished having dinner celebrating the one year anniversary of the night they met. She was starting to clear their dinner dishes when she heard his phone ring. Alex could only hear Dean's end of the call.

"Are you shittin' me?"

"Yeah, I'll tell the guys."

"Yeah, tomorrow works."

"Thanks."

Dean hung up the phone and turned to her with a huge smile on his face.

"Holy shit, we got signed!"

"Oh my god, that's so great."

"I need to be in LA tomorrow. "

"How long will you be gone?"

"No, I mean I'm moving there."

"But, I can't leave."

"I know and I'm sorry but this has always been my dream."

"But, what about us?"

"I can't pass this up."

"I love you. Please don't do this to me."

"This is my dream, what don't you get? It's over."

Alex grabbed her purse and ran out of Dean's house. After she got in her car, she buried her head in her hands and started sobbing. The pain that she felt was almost unbearable. Once she had composed herself enough, she drove home and went right to bed, crying herself to sleep. After Dean left her, she threw herself into her work. That was probably for the better, as she really needed to focus on the farm. It was important that Alex learn all aspects of his business, as she would take over as owner someday. Unfortunately that day came way too soon.

Alex had just celebrated her twenty-first birthday when her father succumbed to his battle with cancer. As much as she tried to prepare herself for his passing, she was still completely devastated. Alex was by his side when he passed. A few minutes after he drew his last breath, Alex came out of his bedroom, tears streaming down her cheeks, and fell to her knees in the middle of her living room.

Her friends helped her up and wrapped her in a group hug as they walked her over to her couch. George and Margie McMillan, the couple that taught her father how to be a farmer sat down on either side of her and tried their best to comfort her. She was so grateful for all the support. George took care of making the phone calls that were unfortunately necessary. He and Margie also helped her plan the funeral.

The funeral was the hardest thing she ever had to do, but somehow she made it through with the help of those closest to her. She ended up having to extend the viewing for an extra two hours due to the vast amount of people who'd come to pay their last respects. Alex gave the staff two weeks off with pay to give them and herself time to start to heal. She made her whole life about her work to help battle the grief. It certainly helped during the day, but night time was rough. It was so quiet without him there and most nights she ended up crying herself to sleep. Her father was a well-respected member of the community, and she was able to keep those relationships after his passing. Alex found that staying at her childhood farm was too painful, given her father's passing. She was able to sell it for a substantial profit and purchased a larger farm on the other side of town.

Over the years, the pain lessened but never truly went away. Every time Alex heard The Hounds on the radio or TV, every time she saw pictures of Dean in all the rock magazines, she ached. She loved him so much and he just discarded her like day old garbage. How the hell was she ever going to get over him?

Unknown to Alex, Dean was suffering just as much. On the surface, it looked like he was having the time of his life, but deep down, he missed the fuck out of Alex. That woman affected him more than he realized. Once all the glitz and glamour of the music business started wearing off, he desperately wanted to be with her again. He had lost count of how many times he thought about calling her, dreamt about holding her and fucking her. Even when tours brought him to the East Coast, however, he was too afraid of her reaction and he never called her. He just needed to figure out how the fuck to get her out of his system.

After realizing she had been standing there lost in thought for close to an hour, she figured she better get her ass in gear and get some work done.

Alex headed outside to start her daily chores. A few hours into her work, she heard a loud commotion at the farm next door to hers. The previous owner had passed away about a year ago and the farm had remained unsold. She saw a couple of moving trucks. Looks like someone bought the farm next door, finally. Hope I get a decent neighbor, preferably a hot, sexy man, she thought to herself.

Alex had been single most of her adult life. Sure she had some dates and a plenty of one night stands here and there, but nothing in terms of a relationship. An intelligent, successful, fairly attractive woman like me should have no problem finding a relationship. Nope, not this woman. Instead, she was still carrying a torch for the one that got away.

When she arrived back at her house, she sat down on the porch, her mind flooded with memories of the man she who broke her heart and ruined her for all other men. She would have given anything to see him again, to be in his arms again. And holy shit, to get fucked by him again. Nobody had ever made her feel quite like he had. Her mind went back to the night they met, about a month after she lost her father.

Before she upset herself any further, she got up and went back to finishing her work on the farm then went in to grab a shower. She was meeting her friends for lunch, so she certainly couldn't go smelling like the farm. After having no friends as a child, she was grateful to have these women in her life. They were naughty just like her, getting together at their favorite restaurant once a month to discuss the latest trashy novels they were reading, eventually naming themselves 'The Dirty Girl Club.' They would also take turns hosting girls' nights at each others homes.

Once she was finished getting ready, she headed down to their local pizza joint. Debbie and Heather were already there when she arrived and Dee and Jan arrived shortly thereafter. They spent the next couple of hours scarfing down pizza and Pepsi, laughing hysterically and trying to out-naughty each other. She was especially grateful today as it took her mind off the aching she felt from thinking about Dean. After lunch, they all hugged goodbye and headed home.

When Alex was done, she stopped at the grocery store to grab a few things she was out of and grabbed a salad for dinner to balance out eating way too much pizza at lunch earlier. After she ate, she stopped by the stable to feed Midnight and make sure she didn't need anything. She went back to the house to get Holly and grab a book. She walked down to the pond on her property to do some reading. Being outside always helped. After about an hour of reading, she and Holly did a couple laps around the property. It was starting to get dark, so she headed back to the house. As she was walking back, she saw a couple more trucks pull into the farm next door, leaving her wondering again what her new neighbor would be like. Maybe I'll bake something and head over to welcome them, she thought to herself. She shrugged to herself then went inside and watched TV for a few hours before heading to bed.

Chapter Two

Dean Fox arrived in Pennsylvania the morning after the moving
trucks. The bank had arranged to have someone on-site to let
the movers in and lock up behind them. Dean headed right
to the bank to sign the deed, then headed to his brand new home. He
was hoping to catch a glimpse of his new neighbor, but no such luck.
He found himself hoping it was a sexy, single woman. Who was he
kidding, he wanted it to be a certain sexy woman, though he doubted
she would still be single after all these years. He went inside and laid
down on the couch, closed his eyes and started thinking about his life
and what brought him back east.

Dean knew from a young age that he wanted to be a singer. Born
and raised in South Philadelphia, he would sing to anyone, anywhere.
He was always hell on wheels, never caring much about school. For him
it was always music. Besides singing, he was also proficient in drums.
After trying out both, he knew for sure he wanted to be a singer, to be
the one front and center. Once he entered high school, he formed a
band, The Hounds, and started looking for local gigs in Philadelphia
and nearby areas. There were several clubs that allowed under-21 bands
to play, so Dean and his band rotated that circuit. They quickly became
one of the most popular local acts, eventually leading to a record deal.
That was also where he met her.

The Hounds were hired to play at a hot new rock club in Lancaster, Pennsylvania. When it was time for their set, they headed onto the stage, awaiting the curtain rise. Dean took his place front and center and got ready. When the curtain went up, he almost fell off the stage when he saw her. Sitting at the VIP table was an absolute goddess. Her beautiful red hair looked like flames when the spotlight hit it. And holy shit, those were some of the hottest tits he'd ever seen. He noticed her eyes never left him during his entire performance.

While he would like to think he was classy enough to be gazing into her eyes, nope. He couldn't take his eyes off that sexy cleavage spilling out of her tight sexy shirt. All he could think about the whole time was getting her backstage and fucking her after his set. After The Hounds left the stage, they were greeted by the club's owner, Jake. Dean asked him if he would ask the beautiful girl at the VIP table to come backstage so they could meet. He returned a few minutes later with his goddess in tow. It was then that Dean saw how tall and curvy she truly was.

Jake knocked on the dressing door, which Dean answered nearly naked, loving that her eyes went right to his package. She was completely starstruck by him, which definitely turned him on. Jake introduced her as Alexandra. He invited her into his dressing room and before long she was naked and sitting on his cock. Fuck, that was one hot pussy he thought as her huge tits bounced in his face. After he filled her pussy full of cum, she just sat in his lap, his cock still stuffing her, just gazing at him.

After a few minutes, they got dressed and headed to a local diner to get some food. They ended up talking for hours, getting to know each other. It wasn't long before they were in a relationship, fucking as much as possible. Dean thought this was true love, and that she was the one. That is until he got the news he'd always been waiting for, being signed to a label. He had to tell her he was leaving. It hurt but in the end, music was his dream and he wouldn't let anything get in the way. They parted on bitter terms and that was the last he ever spoke to her.

The record company flew the band to LA. They immediately went into the studio and recorded their first album. The album was a success but Dean was never truly satisfied with it. The record company and the band's manager quickly made it clear they owned them. The songs, their image, everything about them was dictated by the record company. They even went so far as to tell them what type of woman would be most desirable. They were young and blinded by all the money the record company was throwing their way, so they never tried to resist. Dean was never with a petite blond on his arm, but secretly, he always had a thing for red-heads. He also preferred a curvier woman, especially in the chest area, not these little waifs they kept telling him to date.

As he got older, Dean's priorities started shifting. He had more than enough money for the rest of his life, but felt he had nothing to show for it. Not one song he ever recorded and released was written by him. His image certainly wasn't what he wanted. Dean was a country boy at heart, not the city slicker they turned him into. He hated leather and button-down shirts, and would have traded them for jeans and a t-shirt if he could have. He could feel himself growing more and more restless, and starting to have thoughts about leaving the music business.

Dean put those plans on hold when the record company informed him they booked The Hounds on a six-month worldwide tour to celebrate twenty-five years of success. Every venue he was booked to play was completely sold out and the fans were incredible. Seeing the reaction from the people rekindled Dean's love for music, and he decided to stick it out a while longer. All of that would change when he arrived back in LA.

Dean was able to catch an early flight and arrived home sooner than he had planned. He was going to call Zoe and tell her but decided to surprise her. Instead, Dean was the one who was in for a surprise. He walked upstairs to their bedroom and found Zoe in their bed, fucking his now-former manager Danny. The door was partially closed, so Dean slammed it open.

"You have five fucking seconds to get the fuck out of my house."

Zoe quickly climbed off of Danny.

"I-I-I thought you were coming home tomorrow, baby," Zoe stammered.

"Don't fucking 'baby' me, you whore. You couldn't keep your fucking legs closed while I was gone. I was ecstatic at how well the tour went, so I got an earlier flight to come home and celebrate with you.

This is what I get, you fucking my asshole manager. By the way, Danny, you're fired. Now, as I just said, GET THE FUCK OUT."

Zoe and Danny quickly dressed and ran out of Dean's house. Dean was so distraught, he went downstairs and downed an entire bottle of whiskey, then passed out on his couch. He woke up the following morning feeling like shit, both from his hangover and his breakup. That was the nail in the coffin and he knew what he had to do.

"Not only do I need to leave the music business, I need to leave LA," he said out loud to nobody.

And leave LA, he did. The next day, he called his real estate agent, who put his house on the market. His agent also helped him find a new home. He decided there was no place like home, so he moved back to Pennsylvania. He loved that while there was a downtown urban area, there were also many rural areas. Dean knew this was what he wanted. Living somewhere rural would afford him the privacy he was so desperately seeking. In looking at the real estate listings, he stumbled upon a large farm for sale.

The owner had passed and had no heirs, so the property went back to the bank. Dean knew from the pictures that this was the place for him, so he put in an offer. The property value was on the higher side, but that wasn't an issue for him. As he was able to pay cash, and because it had been a year with no previous offers, the bank quickly accepted his offer. Dean wrote a post on his social media, announcing to the world that he was leaving music forever, then deactivated his account. Two days later, he had all of his belongings packed. The movers loaded everything and departed for Pennsylvania.

Dean had one final thing to take care of the next day, then he would be bidding farewell to LA forever. He had always hated his sports car and only owned it to maintain his image, but that was over. Secretly, he was always a pickup truck kinda guy, so he traded the car in for a brand new Ford truck. Once he finished signing all the paperwork, he started his journey. Not only was he moving to a new home in a new state, but he was also starting a new life. Not my new life, he corrected himself, my true life. This was the happiest he had been in a long time, and it felt fucking amazing.

When finally arrived at his home, he took a walk around to see it in person. He had only seen pictures, but was happy with what he saw. There was an extra barn off to the side of the property that he planned on turning into a recording studio. Plus, his friend Chris had done an in person inspection and let him know everything was good. His layout was similar to that of Alex's but he had an extra bathroom, added on after the house was built. The second bathroom featured a large soaking tub with jets. If only he had a woman, preferably Alex, to sit in there with. He started wondering where she could be these days and what her life was like.

It was Friday night, and Dean really wanted to go out and celebrate, but he was exhausted after his long drive, so he decided to put that off until the next night. Dean located one of the boxes that had sheets and blankets and quickly made his bed. He grabbed a quick shower, then headed straight to bed. Unsure whether it was due to the drive, or the fact he was finally starting the life he always wanted, or a combination of both, Dean had the best night's sleep he had in quite some time.

Dean awoke the following morning, feeling refreshed. After grabbing a shower and getting dressed, he ate a quick breakfast then started unpacking boxes. A few hours into his work, he needed a break and decided to explore his new property. He was hoping to finally see his new neighbor but no luck. He had been able to find out it was a woman but no further information. Maybe she's a gorgeous, single woman. He made a note to do some digging.

With his luck, she was probably another empty-headed bimbo. I could just go over there and introduce myself, he thought to himself. After what Zoe had done to him though, Dean was not ready to deal with another woman, unless it was one particular goddess. He went back inside his house to unpack more boxes and start getting things organized.

It was close to dinnertime when Dean decided to stop for the night. After a bite to eat, he went upstairs to shower and get dressed. He loved having the freedom to wear whatever he wanted, and opted for his favorite jeans and a black t-shirt from his last tour. He decided to head to the club where he met Alex all those years ago. He doubted she even still lived in the area, but hey, a guy could hope. Despite all the women, all the money, the glitz and glamour of the rock star life, Dean alway felt like something was missing.

More like someone, he thought to himself. He never truly got over her, one of the biggest reasons he was never able to make a relationship work. The long, lonely drive cross-country had given him plenty of time to think. Most of that time was spent thinking about Alexandra. He knew he wanted to see her again, hold her again, fuck her again. He headed back home after a couple of hours at the club. Exhausted from the move and his memories of the love he lost and was so desperate to find, he went to bed.

He woke up the following morning with a huge boner, no surprise after a night of dreaming about fucking his goddess. This many years later and he still wasn't even close to being over her. Fuck I need to find her. Now where to start. After showering and getting dressed, he headed downstairs to have some breakfast then started on his mission to find his beloved. He grabbed his cell phone, dialed a familiar number and when they answered, he said, "Dude, I need your help."

Chapter Three

She woke up the next morning drenched in sweat, as she recalled the dream she had.

She dreamt that she was dressed in a long black evening gown, waiting on her front porch. Suddenly a limo pulled up and, dressed in a black tuxedo, Dean exited the limo. He walked over to her, kissed her passionately then escorted her to the limo. The next thing she knew, they were pulling up at a ballroom and after exiting a limo, walked a red carpet to the cheers of thousands of adoring fans.

All eyes were on them and photographers were trying desperately to get a picture of them. They were escorted to seats in the front row, a large movie screen in front of them. When the movie started playing, it was a biopic of her relationship with Dean. Everyone in the audience was treated to their entire relationship, including all the incredible and dirty sex they'd had. The entire audience was cheering loudly as they watched, but in the dreamworld, it never occurred to her to mind.

Once the movie was over, ending the way their relationship had, with them breaking up, the audience was angry. They started booing loudly and throwing things at them as they tried to leave. They raced outside but didn't get back in the limo. Suddenly, instead of a beautiful evening gown, Alex was back in her work clothes at her farm. She was dirty and covered in sweat and Dean was now only an image on the side of her barn.

She could see him on stage performing, looking so damn sexy. He was in tight leather pants and a shirt that was completely unbuttoned, showing off that sexy chest of his. The scene quickly changed and he was now surrounded by a bunch of half-naked women, all throwing themselves at him. She could hear him talking to her from the screen.

"Look how much I'm having without you. You were never the one, you just thought you were."

He and the group of women then started laughing and pointing in Alex's direction. The faces of the women started to become clear and she saw that they belonged to the girls in her class that were the meanest to her. They started ordering her around, making her work harder and harder until she finally collapsed in a heap in front of her barn. All she could see and hear was the pointing and laughing, the loudest of it coming from Dean himself. Mercifully her alarm went off soon after, rescuing her from the humiliation she was experiencing. Her heart was racing, mostly from seeing Dean so much. As if she knew Alex needed a friend, Holly jumped onto the bed and laid her head on Alex's stomach. That earned her a couple of absentminded rubs on the head.

She looked into Holly's beautiful brown eyes and asked, "Am I ever going to get the fuck over this guy?"

Feeling disgusting after her sweaty night's sleep, Alex grabbed a shower then a quick breakfast. As she did most weekday, she would be spending the day at the local farmer's market selling the crops she had harvested so far this season. Alex's produce almost always sold out, as she believed in growing only quality fruits and vegetables. The nice weather they'd been having helped draw more tourists to the area, which meant more foot traffic in the market. Alex found that she was selling out even faster this year. She loaded up her car, a roomy SUV, with several boxes of produce then headed out. Once she arrived and unloaded the boxes, she decided to take a walk around and see what other vendors were setup. As she was walking, she thought she saw Chris, Dean's best friend, in the crowd but when she looked again, nobody was there but a group of seniors from the local retirement community.

Great, not only am I dreaming about him, now I'm hallucinating too. For fuck's sake, I need to get over him. She walked a little further and saw a new vendor in this year's lineup. Much to her delight, he was peddling used vinyl, mostly rock, her favorite genre. She headed into the shop and started looking through the bins. She had pulled out several records not already in her collection when she heard a male voice behind her.

"You have good taste."

"Thank you."

"I'm Tyler, owner of this booth."

"Alex, owner of Second Shot Farms. I have a booth on the first aisle."

"Nice to meet you."

"Nice to meet you too."

"Feel free to browse as long as you would like."

"Thanks. I could get lost in here. Nothing will ever compare to vinyl."

"Amen, girl. Hey, I hope this isn't too forward, but I was going to close for a bit and grab some lunch. Would you care to join me?"

"I'm getting hungry, so sure. Do you want me to pay for this first?"

"No need, I'll leave them on the counter in case you want to look more after lunch."

"Cool."

They headed down to the food area and each ordered a sandwich and drink. They chatted, mostly about music, while they ate. She always loved finding other people who were into the same kind of music as her. Before they knew it, an hour had passed and Tyler needed to reopen his booth. They headed back so Alex could finish looking through his inventory. When she was done, she headed up to the counter to pay for everything. After saying goodbye to Tyler, she headed back to her booth to give it a thorough cleaning then head home for the day. She was so engrossed in her work, she never saw noticed someone watching her.

When she got home, she checked in on her workers and helped them organize the crops they had harvested that day. She then headed out to the hen house to collect any eggs they had laid. Alex loved the farm life, especially her animals and she made sure that she was ethical in her work. She hated seeing stories about higher producing farms that left their animals in conditions that diminished their quality of life. She took a couple of courses to ensure that she was always doing things in the best interest of the animals. She also stayed away from any parts of farming the required the killing of animals. This was a big part of why her business was so successful.

After a few hours, Alex headed to her house to grab a shower, as the girls were coming over for dinner and an adult sleepover. She loved getting the chance to cook for her friends and hang out with them. It definitely helped with the loneliness of not having a man. After her shower, she put the lasagna in the oven and set the table. The girls arrived about half an hour later. They sat at the table and drank wine until the lasagna was ready. They finished off the whole thing, plus way too many bottles of wine.

They were a bit tipsy by the time dinner was done and they headed to Alex's living room to watch movies. They were laughing so hard by the end of the movie marathon, their stomachs were aching. After polishing off a couple more bottles of wine, they set up their sleeping bags and drifted off to sleep. Alex, of course, had a fitful night sleep, having more spicy dreams about Dean. Why the hell can't I get him out of my head? She got up and put some coffee on, figuring the other lushes would need some like she did!

The other girls got up shortly after Alex, so she poured them each a cup of coffee and started making breakfast. After breakfast the other girls headed home to get ready for their day while Alex got ready to head down to the market with today's load of produce. She had more with her today, so she hoped she wouldn't sell out as fast. She showered, dressed, loaded up her car and headed out. After bringing her boxes in and setting everything up, she closed and locked the booth, and headed over to chat with Tyler for a couple of minutes before the market opened. About five minutes before the opening, she headed back to her booth to open everything up.

Alex ended up selling out everything by noon. Luckily, she had some great farmhands harvesting for her daily, so she would always have stuff to sell. She packed up early and headed home to do some baking and add that to what she was selling.

After making herself a quick lunch, she got started on baking. She worked until dinnertime and had quite a few cakes and pies to take with her. She was lucky enough to have a huge kitchen and had two over-sized ovens, so she could bake several things at once. After boxing and refrigerating everything and cleaning, Alex was feeling restless and decided to head to the club to see who was performing. She got a table right down front, and ordered a burger while she waited.

As soon as the opening band hit the stage, Alex felt herself transport back in time. She replayed that night over and over again in her mind. She found the dull ache that always existed in her stomach was growing more intense the more she thought about Dean. She couldn't help hoping that he was as miserable as she was. But how could he be with all those women always draped all over him.

Alex woke up drenched in sweat again. As she showered and got ready for her day at the market, she couldn't help but wonder if her dreams were trying to tell her something. Yeah, she thought, they're telling me I need to get the fuck over this guy once and for all or I'm going to lose my mind. He made his choice and I wasn't it, so why couldn't I stop pining and find a man who actually wanted to be with me?

She arrived at the market and had just finished unloading and setting up when she Tyler heading over. He ended up buying a few things from her before he headed over to his booth. As was becoming their tradition, they enjoyed lunch together. Once they were done for the day, Tyler stopped by and asked her if she wanted to hang out. It was nice to have a friend here at the market to hang around with.

"I'm new to the area, so would love it if you could show us around."

"Us?"

"Like you, my household consists of me and a dog, so I thought we could hang out at a dog park or something. I don't know where a lot of places are yet."

"I would love to. Would you like some dinner first? I could fix us something then we could head over to the park."

"Thank you, that would be great."

Alex gave Tyler her address then headed out. He arrived about an hour later. They ate then headed to the dog park. His dog Daisy and got along great with Holly, and the two of them ran and played for hours, while Tyler and Alex sat and chatted. Dusk was approaching so they called the girls in and headed back to their cars. They said goodnight and headed home. Lost in thought, Alex never saw the car following her home.

The next few days flew by, as did the evenings. Alex took Tyler a few places, showing him some of the tourist attractions and other fun things around town. Of course, she saved the best for last. Friday had finally arrived and when Alex was done for the day, she stopped over at Tyler's booth.

"You up for a fun night out?"

"What'd you have in mind?"

"There's an awesome rock club in downtown Lancaster."

"Count me in, girl."

They agreed on a time and Tyler told her he'd pick her up. Her jaw almost hit the ground when she saw him in tight black leather pants and a tight black shirt. She had opted for jeans and a low-cut Iron Maiden t-shirt. All eyes were on them when they entered the club, looking like a rock star and his woman. They spent most of the night on the dance floor, their inhibitions fading somewhat after a couple of beers each. When they'd had enough, Tyler drove her home.

"I had a great time tonight. It's nice to finally have a friend here."

"I had a great time too. I needed a chance to unwind."

"Do you have any plans for the weekend?"

"Yes. I have desperately been in need of a beach weekend, so I'm heading to Jersey. I rented a two-bedroom house and it is pet-friendly, if you wanted to tag along."

"I love the beach so count me in."

"Awesome, I would love the company. I'll pick you and Daisy up around 7 tomorrow morning if that's not too early."

"I'm used to being up because of the market, so that sounds perfect."

"Cool. There's a cafe I always stop for breakfast because they allow dogs at their outside tables, so we can eat breakfast on the way."

"Sounds like a plan. I'm going to head home and get packed. See you in the morning."

"See you then."

Alex got up the next morning, packed up her car and headed over to pick up Tyler and Daisy. Tyler insisted on paying for breakfast as a small thank you for letting him tag along. Once they got settled, they headed down to the beach with the dogs. Alex always made a point to only rent a house on the beaches that allowed dogs. The took the dogs for a nice long walk then headed back to relax. Holly and Daisy slept cuddled together, completely spent from the walk while she and Tyler sat and talked.

"So, tell me Alex, how come you never mention your relationship?"

"What relationship?"

"Don't even try to tell me you don't have someone special."

"You're looking at her," she said, pointing at Holly.

"A beauty like you?"

"You're sweet. I had someone once, but his dreams didn't include me. Do you remember The Hounds?"

"Of course, they were one of my favorites."

"My boyfriend was Dean Fox. At least he was my boyfriend up until they got a record deal. After that, he didn't need me anymore and off to LA he went. My heart was shattered and I've never quite gotten over him. But life goes on I guess."

"I'm so sorry that someone did that to you."

"Thanks. I've tried like hell to get over him, but so far no luck. It's why I've never been able to keep a relationship. Enough about me though. Tell me something about you."

Tyler looked uncomfortable for a minute. Alex wondered what that was all about. She didn't ask him anything specific, but he seemed hesitant to share. She didn't say anything else, as she didn't want to seem pushy or like she was digging for dirt or anything. After a couple of minutes, he finally answered.

"I had some relationship trouble myself, so I decided to move here for a fresh start."

He didn't offer any details, and after the way he looked earlier, Alex didn't feel right asking.

"Sorry to hear that. I know how bad that sucks. We can be each other's support system to get through it."

Tyler seemed more comfortable hearing that and he smiled.

"Thank you. I'm glad you stopped by my shop that morning. I've enjoyed becoming friends."

"Me too."

The dogs started stirring from their nap and Alex noticed she was getting hungry. She took hold of both leashes so the dogs didn't jump up and take off. She looked over at Tyler, who was just sitting and staring out at the ocean. She couldn't help but wonder what secrets he had, as they seemed to bring him pain.

"How about we take a walk down the boardwalk and grab a slice? I'm a little bit hungry."

"Nothing beats boardwalk pizza. Let's go."

The rest of the weekend flew by and before she knew it, they were back in Lancaster. After dropping Tyler and Daisy off, Alex headed home, unpacked her car then headed out to see what her team had harvested and boxed up for her then headed back to the house. She grabbed some dinner and spent the rest of the evening binge-watching her favorite TV show, then headed to bed.

Chapter Four

Dean spent the better part of his week unpacking boxes and organizing all his stuff. He went room by room putting all his clothes and other items away, as well as organizing furniture and doing any decorating that was needed. No matter what room of the house he was in, he would start fantasizing about Alex being there with him. Most of the time they were naked and he was dreaming about fucking her. He missed having that woman in his arms and he would give anything to see her again.

Despite all the success he achieved before leaving the music business behind, he always felt like something was missing. He never knew what it was until he caught Zoe cheating and her aloof attitude about it. Alex would never have done that. All she did was love him and he threw her away like garbage. Even if he did find her, would she give him a second chance? Would she even be available to give him that chance or had she found someone who loved her the way she deserved? The way that he himself was now capable of. But what if it was too late?

When he arrived in Lancaster, he called his childhood best friend, Chris Forester, to enlist his help. Unlike Dean, who left his home state behind for fame and fortune, Chris went on to college and became a lawyer. He had since relocated from Philly to Lancaster to raise his family, and eventually get elected DA for the county. His friendship was the one constant in Dean's life amid all the chaos of the music industry. He was never one to pull any punches so he very loudly told Dean what an ass he was for breaking Alex's heart.

Chris was able to locate Alex's information including where she lived and where she worked. Prior to giving Dean any information or false hope, he kept tabs on her for a few days. He found out she sold her dad's farm and bought her own, as he had passed away when Alex was twenty-one. He also found out she typically sold her produce at the local farmers market. After checking her out a couple of times, he made note that she wasn't wearing a wedding or engagement ring and it didn't appear that she had a serious boyfriend. He did see her with a guy who ran one of the other booths, but it seemed like they were just friends.

Part of him wanted to approach Alex and ask her some questions, especially to see if she would ever consider taking Dean back, but he wasn't sure how much Dean wanted him to tell her, so he held off and just made notes of everything he discovered. One thing was for certain, time had been kind to her. She was still just as hot and sexy as she was when Dean started dating her. Friday afternoon rolled around and he had no meetings or anything scheduled, so he took a ride over to Dean's house. Boy was he going to be surprised when he found out he bought the farm right next to hers.

He pulled into Dean's driveway and rang the doorbell. Dean came down a few minutes later, as he had been upstairs unpacking boxes. Chris noticed his friend seemed down.

"What's with the face man?"

"Can't stop thinking about Alex. I definitely fucked up not staying with her."

"I love you man, but yeah, you did. She's actually why I'm here. I have some info for you."

"Anything good?"

"I think you'll find it to be mostly good news."

Chris pointed at the farm next door to Dean's, earning a quizzical look from his friend.

"That's her farm. After you left, her dad got sick and passed away. She ended up selling his farm and buying her own on the other side of town. So, yes, you moved right next door to her. She mostly grows produce and harvests eggs from her chickens, but nothing inhumane. She is famous around the county for being an animal-friendly, ethical farmer. I also discovered she sells her produce as well as some other items at the local farmers market.."

"Holy shit, I can't believe I haven't seen her yet. How does she look?"

"Dude, farm life agrees with her. She is just as smokin' hot as when you two were dating. No sign of any rings and I've never seen a guy hanging around. The only person I saw her interact with besides customers is the owner of one of the other booths and they appear to only be friends."

"I can't believe she's not with anyone."

"Think about it, man. Did you ever get over her?"

"Fuck no."

"Well, maybe she never got over you either. What are you going to do?"

"I have no idea. Part of me wants to just go see her, but what if she doesn't want to see me?"

"Man, the only way you're gonna know is if you go to her."

"I guess I'll need to think about it."

"Don't wait too long. You gave her up once, don't make that same mistake twice."

"Maybe I'll just take the weekend and the decide."

"Not a bad idea. It's a lot to take in."

"It is. Finishing up my unpacking will hopefully keep my mind off of her."

"Speaking of keeping your mind off her, we can hang tomorrow night."

"I don't want to take you away from the family."

"Tracey and the girls will be away for the weekend, so how about an old-fashioned guys night at the club?"

"Exactly what I need."

"Cool. We can grab a bite before. I'll swing by around 6."

"See ya then and thanks for your help with Alex."

"You got it."

After Chris left, Dean headed back inside to do some more unpacking. He worked until almost midnight. Completely exhausted, he headed to bed and as usual, had a very graphic, sexy dream about Alex. *If I wake up with a hard-on one more damn time...*he thought to himself. He got up and showered then went back to working on the house. He kept going non-stop until he needed to get ready for his night out with Chris. He started thinking again about Alex, wondering if he could get lucky enough for her to be at the club too.

As they were on their way, Dean thought about something.

"Is Jake still the club owner?"

"No, his son took over when Jake retired to Florida."

"Okay. I was thinking he might not let me in after I broke Alex's heart."

"If he was, I would have just planned for us to go somewhere else, but no worries."

When they got to the club, the parking lot was close to full as was the inside. Chris had a table reserved so they were able to get right in. The perks of being the DA. They downed a few beers and hung at their table, turning away several women who were definitely interested. Dean didn't want to do anything that could possibly jeopardize anything with Alex. He kept an eye on the door all night, but no sign of her.

They headed out around 11 and drove past Alex's house to head home. The house was completely dark so she either wasn't home or had already gone to bed. Dean started thinking he might try again tomorrow to head over, but he wasn't sure. Chris took him home from there. Dean couldn't sleep when he got inside so he put the TV on, but that wasn't helping either so he headed to his music room and started writing.

Fuck, I miss her so much. I would give just about anything to have that woman in my arms again. He ended up writing for a couple of hours until he finally started feeling tired. The song quickly turned into a love song about Alex. He headed off to bed and like the night before, his dreams were filled of images of Alex, but not naughty this time. This time, the dream was more tender, as if their love had never gone away. He woke up with an agonizing aching in his stomach. He knew for sure what he had to do. He had to go see her, he had to know whether they had a chance or if it was completely over. The latter would be difficult but not as difficult as the unknown.

Dean couldn't believe it was already Sunday. He figured one more day would be enough to get everything unpacked and organized. The last few boxes he had left were for his bedroom. When he got done, he realized he had a whole dresser that was empty. He didn't have any less stuff, so he couldn't figure out why he did that. Maybe, I left it open for Alex, he thought. Fuck, is there anything I do that doesn't involve her? He decided to take a walk outside to clear his mind. He had just stepped out onto his front porch when he saw her car pulling up in front of her house. He stood there watching as she got out of her car and holy shit, his heart started racing. Damn, I still love that woman, he thought to himself.

He quickly ducked back inside before she saw him. He didn't yet know if she knew he was back and especially if she knew he was that close. He sat down on the couch again remembering all the good times they had before he left. The longer he sat there, the more determined he was to go see her. He decided not to go to her house, but instead he would head down to the market tomorrow and see her there. He still wasn't sure he would have the guts to talk to her or even if she would want him to but he at least wanted to see her upclose. HIs reverie was interrupted by his cell phone ringing.

"Hey Chris."

"Hey, Tracey's going to be away for one more night, so how about you head over for dinner? I'll throw some burgers or something on grill."

"Sounds good. I have some shit to run by you anyway."

"Alex-related, I assume?"

"Yeah."

"See you at 5?"

"See you then."

After they disconnected, Dean ran out to the local beverage place and grabbed a case of Chris's favorite beer. He was grateful to have his friend here to help him sort out everything with Alex. His mind was a jumbled mess right now, so Chris with his clear head, should be able to help him sort everything out. When he got back home, he put the beer in a cooler with some ice so it would have time to chill before he headed over to Chris's house. With some time to kill before he had to leave, he sat down to write more of the song he started about Alex, which did nothing to help settle his thoughts.

Around 4:30, he loaded up the cooler and headed to Chris's. After a quick tour, they headed out back and Chris threw the burgers on while they each enjoyed a cold beer.

"I saw Alex today."

"Where?"

"I went outside and saw her pull into her driveway and get out of her car."

"She see you?"

"I went back in before she did."

"How was it seeing her after all this time?"

"I realized how much I still loved her. I also decided I'm going to see her tomorrow."

"Where?"

"I'm going to head down to the farmers market near closing time and stop by her booth."

"Good luck, dude. You know I hope it works out for you guys."

"Thanks man."

After they ate and had a couple more beers, they shot the shit for a couple of hours. Chris had some work to do to get ready for court in the morning, so Dean headed home. He worked some more on the song then went to bed early. He wanted to be well-rested and clear-headed for what was going to be an interesting day. The next morning, he got up feeling the best he had since he got back. He kept himself busy all day, trying not to get too worked up about Alex. He knew the market closed at 5, so he left about a half-hour before to head down.

When he arrived, he walked around until he found the booth he was looking for. His heart leapt into his throat when he saw his goddess. She had her back to the entrance, cleaning so she didn't see him approach. After struggling for a few minutes to find his voice, he summoned up the courage.

"Hi, Alex."

Chapter Five

Alex stopped dead in her tracks when she heard that voice say her name. It couldn't be, she thought, as her eyes filled with tears. She slowly turned around and found herself face-to-face with Dean. She couldn't find her voice, and just stood there gaping at him. After a few minutes, she recovered, but she had no idea what to say. Everything sounded lame.

"Hi, Dean."

That was all it took and the tears came spilling out, leaving her feeling like a fool. Dean started to approach her she shook her head no and put her hand up, so he stopped.

"What are you doing here?"

"I left LA for good and moved back here. I've been here about a week."

"Oh."

"I bought the farm next to yours."

"Why the hell did you do that?"

"I didn't know it was you I was moving next to."

"How did you find me?"

"Chris."

"Oh."

"Can we please go somewhere and talk?"

"Why the fuck should I? You left me."

"Please, baby. Let me explain."

"Give me one good reason why I should."

"Because I never stopped loving you."

"Then why the fuck did you leave me?"

"I thought music was my dream, but what I realized is that you were actually my dream."

"You expect me to believe that? I see what you have. Money, fame, fortune, women whenever you want."

"I left it all behind."

"Why?"

"Because something was always missing."

"What?"

"You."

Alex didn't know what to say to that. She desperately wanted to tell Dean that she had never gotten over him, but she held back for now. She first needed to know what his intentions were before she said anything.

"What do you want from me?"

"Can we go to dinner and talk?"

"I'm not sure that's a good idea."

"Please, Alex, just hear me out."

"Okay. I just need to finish cleaning up and carry everything out to my car."

"I'll help."

He helped her pack up her stuff and carry everything outside. They agreed to meet at the local diner where they ate the night they met at the club. Dean followed her over to make sure she didn't change her mind. He was so thankful she had agreed, even if reluctantly, and he didn't want to risk her thinking better of it. They parked next to each other and headed in, picking a somewhat private table in the corner.

"Thank you for agreeing to hear me out."

"Don't get too excited. I'm mostly just curious why you felt music was more important than me."

"I promise you it wasn't that at all."

"Then what? I loved you."

"I know and I loved you too. Still do. It's just that music had always been my dream. I saw that contract and what they were offering to pay us and I lost sight of anything else, anyone else and not a day has passed that I haven't regretted it."

"You shattered my heart when you left me, I hope you understand that."

"I do."

"I never got over you. I've never been able to make one relationship work even a little bit."

"Me either."

She was starting to soften a bit, but cautiously so. She had to make sure this wasn't just a phase. If she let Dean back into her life, losing him again would be too much.

"So, why did you decide to leave music?"

"It wasn't so much music I left but everything that went with it. LA just wasn't the place for me anymore."

"Even after the tour you guys just finished?"

"You've been keeping up on my career?"

"Of course. I never stopped loving you, Dean."

"Same here."

"So what made you leave and is it really for good?"

"When I got home, I caught the woman I was seeing in bed with my now ex-manager. I was already getting disgusted and that was just the final straw. I knew the only place for me was back here."

"I'm so sorry that happened."

"I deserved it for what I put you through."

"Don't say that. I know things didn't end well with us, but that doesn't mean you didn't deserve happiness."

"I could have that happiness again, but only if it's with you."

"I can't."

"Baby, why not? We love each other."

"I know, but we can't just act like nothing happened. A lot of years have passed. WE've changed, our lives have changed."

"But our love hasn't. Please, give me a chance to prove myself."

"I can't. I'm sorry."

"Please, baby. I would give anything to have you in my arms again."

Alex wanted nothing more. It had been way too long since she'd been with anyone where it actually meant something. But how could she just hop back into bed with him? She sure as hell wanted too though.

"I need time to think. This is a lot to have dumped in my lap out of the blue."

"I understand."

But he didn't understand. He wanted her more than he had ever wanted anyone or anything. He just needed to make her realize she wanted it too, but he knew he couldn't push too hard or he'd lose her for good. They finished eating and got up to pay the check. Alex tried to pay half, but Dean would hear nothing of it. They both walked outside to head home.

"Please just give me time to digest all this."

Dean nodded but he had other ideas. He followed Alex, but she thought nothing of it since they lived so close. When she pulled into her driveway, Dean pulled in behind her. When she got out of her car, he did the same and walked over to her. Without uttering a word, he pulled her into his arms and kissed with the passion she remembered. She started kissing him back but then abruptly pulled away.

"What's wrong?"

"You can't just come waltzing back into my life and expect everything to pick up where we left it."

"Why not?"

"It doesn't work like that. Do you have any idea how bad you shattered my heart? I've never been able to fully repair it."

A sad look crossed Dean's face when she said that, almost causing her to regret it. No, she yelled at herself, he's the one that hurt you and he needs to hear this.

"I'm sorry."

"I appreciate that, but you can't expect me to just up and forget."

"But I want to be with you."

"I need time. The best I can give you right now is being friends, but really just casually."

"But that kiss."

"It was amazing, but it doesn't erase everything. Please I just need you to give me time. I can't say how much. I can't even say I'll ever be able to be with you again, but you have to give me time to sort all that out."

Dejectedly, he answered, "Okay."

He turned and headed back to his truck. Before he got in he turned to her and pleaded one last time but she was adamant that she needed time, so he got in his truck and pulled out of her driveway. Her heart told her to run after him but luckily her brain won out and she just stood and watched him go before heading inside. She never noticed the shadowy figure watching her.

She sat down on the couch and buried her head in her hands, tears spilling over. Great, she thought, more tears as a result of this man. She was a jumbled mess of emotions, fueled both by her intense love for Dean, the pain that he had caused her all those years ago and her fear that if she did let him back in, it would lead to another heartbreak and she wasn't sure she could handle that again.

While she sat in her living room, Tyler was quietly sitting in his car. He had just watched that whole scene unfold and he was agitated. Alex was his friend and there's no way that guy was coming back into her life and taking that away from him. He felt a little better when he saw Alex reject him, but how long would that last? She had just told him how she never got over Dean. He would definitely have to keep a closer eye on her. If she started to let Dean back into her life, Tyler would just take care of him like he did the others.

Morning arrived way too quickly, and after another restless night of sleeping, Alex was exhausted but she still got up and got everything ready to head to the market. Lunchtime rolled around and Tyler stopped by to see if she wanted to join him for a quick bite. After they grabbed their lunch and sat down, Tyler looked at his friend.

"Everything okay today? You don't seem like your usual self."

"Yeah, I'm okay."

"I'm here if you need to talk."

"Thanks. Just dealing with some stuff. I appreciate the offer, but I'll be okay."

Tyler was satisfied that she was down, as he took that to mean that things hadn't changed. He would never let Dean get close to her again. Alex was his now, even if she didn't know it. The afternoon was a blur, as Alex's stand was busy as always so she thankfully didn't have time to sit and dwell over Dean. She was getting ready to pack up for the day when Tyler stopped by.

"Do you want to grab some dinner and hang out tonight?"

"I have plans tonight, but thanks for asking."

For a split-second, Alex thought she saw an angry look on Tyler's face but when she looked again, it was gone, so she figured she was just seeing things.

"A quiet night in?"

"No, I'm heading out to meet my friends for dinner and some girl-talk."

Tyler smiled, happy to hear that her plans didn't include Dean. Something still had him feeling restless though, so he decided he would follow her wherever she was going so he could make sure she wasn't lying. He helped her carry her stuff to her car, then walked to his car and waved goodbye to her. He sat down the road from her house, out of sight until he saw her car go by. He waited a few minutes then followed her to the restaurant where she was meeting the girls. He watched her go in then pulled into a spot at the back corner of the lot to wait for her to leave.

When Alex went inside, she approached the seating hostess. Since they dined here often, everyone knew them, so the hostess just pointed to the table where the other girls were and Alex went over to the table. After a quick hug for everyone, she sat down. The girls noticed right away that something was bothering her and made her spill it.

Alex filled them in on what had transpired with Dean, leaving them all looking shocked. They all told her she handled it right and that they would have all done the same thing. She knew it too, but there was something bothering her, though she couldn't put a finger on it. She just hoped she wasn't making a mistake not giving this another try. What if I miss out on my chance? She put those thoughts out of her head for the night and enjoyed a great meal with great friends. She always felt better after spending a couple of hours with the girls, especially when wine was involved. Alex never let herself get too tipsy to drive, but she was at least feeling a little more relaxed.

She was so lost in her thoughts, she never saw the car pull out behind her and follow her most of the way to her house. Tyler had found a place where he could pull over and still be able to see her house, so he did just that. He shut his lights and engine off and watched Alex pull into her driveway and immediately go inside. He remained there until he saw all the lights go off. Satisfied that she was alone, he headed home.

Chapter Six

The next morning, Alex was getting setup for the day at the market when she saw a familiar face come around the corner. She really wasn't ready yet to deal with Dean but she did a little better than she had when he first came back into her life. She had to admit, she was softening a little bit, but she wasn't ready to let him back in completely. Being friends would have to be enough for now.

"Hi, Alex."

"Hey, Dean."

"Need any help today?"

"I'm fine unless you really want to help."

"I would love to."

"Okay. I guess you must be bored"

He smiled but didn't answer. Instead, he helped her finish getting setup and had a little time before customers would be entering the market. Tyler rounded the corner and was not happy when he saw Dean, but he couldn't let Alex know that.

"Good Morning, Alex. And, hey, aren't you rock singer Dean Fox?"

"Yes I am."

"Great to meet you. I'm Tyler and I run the record booth a couple rows over. You should come check it out."

"I would love to but I told Alex I would help her."

"It's okay, Dean, I'm fine. Go check out Tyler's store. He has some great stuff."

Dean and Tyler headed over to his booth, and Alex breathed a sigh of relief. She knew Dean would be back, but at least for now, she could just relax and focus on her sales. She didn't see the guys again until lunchtime when they headed over to see if she wanted to join them. Alex smiled, happy to see the two of them hit it off. They all headed down to the food area. Tyler showed Dean the sandwich stand they always ordered from. Once they got their food, they all sat down together and talked music. As Alex sat and listened to the guys talking, she could feel the slightest crack in the wall she put around her heart. The mere thought of it excited and scared her at the same time.

They headed back when they were done eating, but this time Dean went with Alex. He and Tyler talked about looking through some more records some time this week, which meant that Dean would be around the market more. She told herself she could handle it, but she wasn't completely convinced. She had plenty of experience keeping things in, so she would just bury her feelings behind a smile. Dean showed up every single day, putting more cracks into her wall. She wasn't sure how much longer she would be able to resist. Friday night rolled around and Tyler stopped by when Alex was packing up.

"Getting ready to head out?" Tyler asked.

"Yes, I'm exhausted this week. I had a lot of crops to harvest so I was helping out the team."

"So, I guess the club is out then?"

"Tonight yes, but maybe tomorrow night."

He turned to Dean.

"How about you?"

Dean looked at Alex as if he was asking if it was okay.

"You should go with him. Have a guys night! I'll be better tomorrow after I get some rest."

"Okay, maybe the three of us can hang out tomorrow," Tyler answered.

"I would love to cook for you guys if you want to head over tomorrow night. I'll have plenty of manly-man food on the grill!"

The guys both agreed they would all meet at Alex's house Saturday around 5. She couldn't wait to hear stories about their night at the club. Maybe they'd both meet women and then Alex wouldn't have to worry about what to do about her feelings for Dean. She got up the next morning and headed to the store to get what she needed for dinner then headed home to do any prep. Once she was done with that, she headed out to the farm to take care of anything that needed tending, including making sure she had everything boxed up and ready for a new week at the market.

When she got back to the house, she gave a quick call to Tyler to let him know that Daisy was welcome to join him. Tyler thanked her and disconnected. He was glad to be included so that he could keep an eye on Dean and Alex. He could see her starting to soften towards Dean and he couldn't let that happen. If Dean got too close or if Alex let her heart soften, he might have to have a repeat of last time and he really didn't want it to come to that. She also called Dean and told him that Chris and his family were welcome as she had bought way too much food. Having all those extra people around would help Alex feel more at ease and not focus as much on Dean. She also invited the girls as well. Might as well make a party out of it.

Everybody got there right around the same time. Dean arrived with Chris and his family, the girls all came together and Tyler arrived with Daisy. They all headed out back where Alex had her grill and picnic table. Everyone talked and got to know each other while Alex got the food on. After a few minutes, Dean headed to the grill to help her. They didn't notice Tyler glaring at they them as they talked and laughed as they worked. He was starting to formulate a plan in his head that he feared he would have to enact like so many times before. So much for a fresh start, he thought to himself. Once the cooking was done, Alex and Dean carried everything over to the table.

Everyone had come equipped with a hearty appetite so Alex didn't have a lot left over. Daisy and Holly kept making the rounds looking for anyone to drop anything, especially of the meat variety. After dinner, Chris's girls asked if they could take the dogs for a walk. Chris showed them where they could go so he could keep an eye on them. While they were gone, Alex started cleaning everything up. Once dusk was approaching, Alex built a fire in her fire pit so everyone could toast up some marshmallows and make s'mores for dessert.

After dessert, the little ones were getting tired so Chris and Tracey started packing up their stuff. Dean walked over to help him and Tyler saw him whisper something to Chris then rejoin the group.

Once the girls' stuff was all packed, Chris walked over to where Alex and Dean were standing.

"Thank you so much for having us, Alex. Dean, I hate to do this, but would you be able to catch a ride with someone else, so I can get the girls home?"

"I don't live that far, so I can walk."

"Thanks, buddy."

"No problem."

Alex's friends headed out shortly after Chris, leaving just Alex, Dean, and Tyler. Tyler got Daisy all packed up and put her and her stuff in his car.

"Can I give you a lift, Dean?"

"Thanks but I'm going to stay and help Alex finish cleaning up. Thanks for the offer though."

"No problem."

Tyler hesitated for a minute then got in his car. He watched Alex and Dean standing there gazing at each other and he wasn't happy, so he headed to his hiding spot. He wanted to see how long Dean stayed. After he finished helping Alex cleanup, they got in her car so she could take him home. Tyler moved far enough off the road that they never noticed his car. He stayed there until Alex was back home and all her lights were out for the night. He decided he would keep an eye on them again this week and have his plan ready in case he needed it. Nobody was taking his Alex away from him.

After Alex dropped him off, Dean headed up to bed but he couldn't sleep. He felt like Alex was starting to open her heart up to him a little bit and he loved how it felt. They had a great time laughing and talking while they were grilling. She even gave him a hug when she dropped him off, sending his heart into overdrive. He had to keep it contained a bit as he didn't want to push too hard. He looked over at the empty side of the bed wishing that Alex was laying there next to him like she used to.

Of course, they would both be naked after another round of incredible sex. He would give anything to be with her again, but for now, he would settle for being friends.

Alex wasn't doing much better. She laid there staring at her ceiling, remembering the kiss she and Dean shared and how she really wanted to take it further. Before she could though, she had to make sure this was real. She knew there were no guarantees but she also didn't want to jump in the deep end only to have Dean up and leave her again. What if he realized the missed LA and the industry and went back, again leaving her behind. As much as she would give anything to have Dean in her bed again, she just wasn't ready.

Alex woke up the next morning exhausted from another restless night, so she decided a nice quiet Sunday was just what she needed. She grabbed some breakfast then took Holly for a long walk around her property. That always seemed to clear head and she loved their time together. She got back a couple hours later and laid down on the couch to watch some TV, and was asleep within about five minutes. She woke up a couple hours later when she heard a car coming up her driveway. What was Tyler doing here, she thought to herself. She walked outside to see what was up.

He got out of his car and walked to where she was standing.

"Wanted to see if you wanted to hang out today."

"I'm taking today just to relax and unwind before another busy week."

"Fine."

"Hey, don't be like that."

"I thought we were friends."

"We are, I just need a day to myself. It's nothing against you."

"Whatever."

Without another word, he got back in his car and took off, leaving her standing there in stunned silence. What the hell was that about? She certainly hadn't meant to be rude and didn't think that she was. She would try talking to him at the market in the morning and see if there was something she did that upset him. Until then, she put the encounter out of her head and went back inside.

Unlike her, Tyler couldn't put it out of his mind. He figured she must be hanging out with Dean and was just trying to push him out of the picture. Well, he wouldn't let that happen. He drove to where he knew he could get his hands on drugs and bought a bag of roofies. It looked like it might be time to put his plan into action, so he needed to make sure everything was ready. Once he had everything he needed, he returned to his lookout spot to make sure Alex was alone for the rest of the night like she told him she would be. He never saw any activity other then her taking Holly outside a couple of times, but still he sat there for hours just watching until her lights went out for the night.

Alex headed up to bed and had herself another restless night's sleep, though this time it wasn't because of Dean. She had a bad dream about something being taken away from her, though she couldn't see anyone or anything specific, which made it even scarier. She woke in a cold sweat, and with her heart racing. She got up and got ready to head into the market unable to shake the uneasy feeling the dream left her with.

Chapter Seven

A lex got to the market a little earlier than usual as she had more to set up, plus she wanted a chance to talk to Tyler before the market opened. She put her stuff down and walked to his booth but he wasn't there yet, so she went back to get her stuff ready. About ten minutes, she saw Tyler walking in so she stopped him.

"I wanted to apologize about yesterday. I didn't mean to offend you. I just needed a quiet day to myself."

"I'm the one who owes you an apology. You've been such a good friend to me and I should have respected your wish.

"Thank you. The day alone was just what I needed. This is the most energized I've felt in a while."

Suddenly, he saw Alex look to her left and her face lit up like a Christmas tree. He glanced over and immediately felt an intense anger in his gut. He took a deep breath to ward it off as his nemesis Dean was approaching. He certainly did not like the reaction from Alex when she saw him. He knew Dean was now a threat and he had to be dealt with. But in order for that to happen, Tyler couldn't let on that he was angry.

"Since we didn't get to this past weekend, how about the three of us hit the club on Friday night to unwind," Tyler suggested.

Dean and Alex both agreed that sounded like fun, so they firmed up a time to meet. Dean had some more records he wanted to look through so he headed over with Tyler to open his booth while Alex got ready for another busy day of selling her produce. The market seemed busier today and she was already running low by lunchtime. She didn't want to miss out by closing early so she had one of her farmhands deliver some more boxes so she could restock.

The rest of the week was pretty much the same. Alex never even got a chance to break for lunch any day that week, so Dean would run down and bring her something back. He would give her a few minutes to eat while he ran her booth for her. His help was exactly what she needed when she had a week like this. As she watched him working there with her day after day, he walls were coming down a lot faster than she would have wanted, but she couldn't help it. By Thursday afternoon, she knew she was ready to give him a second chance. As they were cleaning up, she managed to find enough courage to say something.

"Thank you so much for your help this week. I was thinking that maybe Saturday night we could try a date. I mean if you want to."

"Of course I want to. I can't tell you how happy I am."

Unfortunately, not everyone was happy about that. Tyler had heard the exchange and he knew it was now time. Dean had to be dealt with. It wouldn't be exactly like before, but it would ensure Alex would never speak to him again. He walked up to them on his way out and addressed Dean.

"How about we hit guys night at the bar tonight? Unless you have plans with this lovely lady, of course."

Like before, he looked at Alex before answering. She didn't jump in so he answered.

"Sure, sounds good. What time do you want to meet?"

"I'll come pick you up around 6."

"Okay."

"You boys have fun. I'm going to be in the kitchen baking some homemade bread to sell tomorrow. See you both in the morning, hopefully not hung over," she said with a smile.

Dean and Tyler both smiled back, but with very different emotions behind those smiles. The three of them walked outside together, with only Tyler knowing what was going to happen later. Once that was done, he would have his woman all to himself. While she was in her kitchen baking and listening to Dean's albums, she was overwhelmed by all those old feelings returning and she was even more confident in giving things another try. She couldn't wait to tell him when they went out on Saturday night.

Meanwhile, Tyler was just pulling into Dean's driveway to pick him up. They headed to the bar and found a table. They each ordered a burger and a beer, then sat and watched the baseball game while they ate. They ordered a couple more rounds of beers. After a few hours, Dean ran to the men's room, giving Tyler the chance to put his plan into action. He slipped a couple of roofies into Dean's beer. Once he started feeling the effects, Tyler walked him out of the bar. Nobody even blinked an eye as they went by, just assuming he'd had too much to drink and needed help to walk out. He put Dean into the passenger seat of his car and started driving down route 222 heading to Stroudsburg, Pennsylvania.

He arrived about two hours later and found an abandoned farm. He took Dean's phone out of his pocket, pulled him out of the car, and laid him down in the yard. Tyler then got back in his car and took off back to Lancaster. He headed straight home, knowing he didn't have to keep an eye on Alex tonight. He knew it would be at least twelve hours before Dean started to come to. He would have no idea where he was and no phone to call for help. He would just have to act like nothing was wrong when he saw Alex. He had a plan for that too. He would put enough doubt in her head that she would never trust Dean again.

Once Alex finished her baking, she headed to bed and quickly fell asleep. She awoke a few minutes later, startled as she saw the ground getting further and further away. The hawk she was riding was soaring through the night sky, wings flapping loudly. She had no idea where she was going or how she got here. They flew a little while longer then suddenly, the hawk stopped and spoke to her, his voice sounding like that of her father.

"My sweet daughter, someone needs you."

"Who, daddy?"

"Look down."

Alex looked down and saw Dean. He looked like he was in some kind of trouble.

"Take me to him."

"I can't."

"Why not?"

"You have to find him first."

"How?"

"I can't tell you that, my child."

Before she could say another word, the hawk flew away, leaving her standing there alone, until she heard a loud beeping noise. Alex woke up with a start when her alarm went off. She felt unsettled after the dream she just had. She tried shaking if off like the night before, but this time the feeling was stronger. She would deal with that later, but for now, she got ready to head down to the market. When she arrived, she unloaded her car and took everything inside to get setup. She kept looking for Dean but even by mid-morning, there was no sign of him. She was lost in thought and starting to get worried when Tyler approached her booth.

"Up for some lunch."

"Oh, yeah, I guess."

"Everything okay?"

"Yep, just surprised Dean hasn't been by yet."

"He had more than his share of beer, maybe he's sleeping off a hangover."

Now Alex was really worried, but she didn't let on. If there was one thing she knew about Dean, it was that while he enjoyed a beer, he always knew his limit. She didn't mention that to Tyler, and instead headed down to lunch with him. After they got their food and found a table, she sighed audibly.

"Talk to me."

"I'm finally starting to feel better about Dean being here. I just hope him not coming in this morning doesn't mean he changed his mind about me. I guess we'll see what happens tonight."

"What happens if he stands us up tonight?"

"To me, that's him saying he's no longer interested in me. That will be the end of things as far as I'm concerned."

Tyler started to smile, unable to control his joy, but he quickly replaced it with a concerned look. He hoped Alex didn't see his slip-up.

He was so close to having what he wanted that he couldn't afford to be careless now. Unfortunately for him, Alex did see it and it sent chills up her spine. She spent the rest of the day serving her customers with her usual sunny disposition, but her insides were a mess. When she had a break, she called Dean's cell. She swore she could hear his ringtone, but just faintly. She got excited, thinking he was here. So closed her booth for a moment and started to look for him. As she approached Tyler's booth, the sound got louder. She disconnected, thinking he was looking at records, but nobody was in Tyler's booth, so she quickly returned to hers.

She knew for sure she wasn't going to the club tonight if Dean wasn't with her. She had a really uneasy feeling about Tyler, especially since as far as she knew, he was the last one who'd seen Dean. When Tyler stopped by her booth, she pretended like everything was fine. If she couldn't reach Dean when she got home, she was going to call Tyler and tell him she wasn't feeling well and just wanted to stay home. They headed out to their cars together to head home.

"See you tonight, Alex."

"Looking forward to it."

As soon as Alex got home, she tried calling Dean over and over and nothing. She had moved on from uneasy to scared. She called Tyler and let him know she felt like she was coming down with something and was going to stay home. She then dialed Chris, in full panic mode.

"Hello."

"It's Alex. Something's wrong."

"What's going on? You sound panicked."

"Something happened to Dean."

"What?"

"I don't know. Please just get here."

Chris jumped in his car and raced over. Alex was waiting at her front door. Chris came in and put his hands on her shoulders to try and calm her down.

"Take a deep breath and tell me what happened."

"Last night, Tyler and Dean went down to the bar for guys night. Then this morning, Dean is a no-show at the market. He's been coming every day and helping me. When I mentioned my concern to Tyler, he blew it off saying Dean had a few too many and was probably sleeping off a hangover. You and I both know he would never drink that much."

Chris nodded, now visibly concerned, as Alex continued.

"The three of us were supposed to hit the club tonight. Tyler asked me what I would do if Dean was a no-show for that too. When I told him that would tell me that Dean no longer wanted me and that it would be the end for me, I caught him smile. It sent shivers down my spine. He quickly tried to cover it up, but I had already seen it."

"I knew something seemed off with him the other night, but you and Dean seemed comfortable so I didn't say anything. Now I wish I had."

"It's not your fault. But, Chris, we need to find him. There's one more thing I need to tell you and this is what has me the most scared. I tried calling his cell this afternoon and I swore I could hear it ringing so I thought he was at Tyler's booth. When I got over there, the ringing got louder, so his phone was there somewhere. I quickly disconnected and went back to my booth before Tyler saw it was me."

"We need to go. Now."

Alex called one of her farm hands to take care of Holly while she ran out. They got in Chris's car and took off for his house. They arrived and headed right for his office. Tracey followed them in and Chris filled her in as he started up his laptop. He searched the DMV database and found what information he could on Tyler. After doing some digging, he found that Tyler had changed his name after some legal trouble but couldn't find anything specific. He called one his judge buddies and was able to call in a favor to secure a warrant to check Tyler's phone.

The internal GPS showed them leaving the bar and heading to Stroudsburg. Chris then called the bar, who reviewed surveillance from the night before. They saw Dean head to the restroom and while he was gone, Tyler put some kind of pills in his drink. Alex was so scared, she was shaking and tears were streaming down her face. Tracey was trying unsuccessfully to calm her down.

"Dean and I had plans to go on a date tomorrow night and I was going to tell him I was ready to try rekindling our relationship. What if I never get that chance now? This is all my fault."

"Come on, we're going to start following the route that they drove and see if we can find him."

They got into Chris's car and started driving. Unsure how long the effects might last and whether Dean was still where Tyler left him might make this a challenge, but no way they would give up. They pulled over at the spot where the GPS showed he had stopped for an extended time, but no sign of Dean. Chris decided to keep driving straight along the highway, hoping that's where Dean would have walked. After nearly six hours of driving, he could see Alex getting more and more upset. Tears were streaming down her face and she was shaking uncontrollably.

"I know this is scary, but we aren't giving up. We will find him."

She couldn't speak, so she just nodded. After about another hour of driving, he heard Alex gasp. She pointed towards the bus stop up ahead, where a man was sitting, his head in his hands. They could tell by his hair it was him, plus Alex had seen him the day he went missing and knew what he was wearing. Chris sped up until they reached the bench, parked and got out. Dean already looked confused, and became even more so when they pulled up.

"Where am I?'

Alex still couldn't talk so Chris answered.

"You're in Stroudsburg. Tyler dropped you off here."

"I don't understand."

"Neither do we. We just know that he slipped you something at the bar."

"What?"

"We're not sure, so we need to get you to a hospital."

"I don't wanna. I just wanna go home."

"I know, buddy, but we need to know exactly what we're dealing with."

Dean looked over at Alex, who nodded in agreement. Chris looked up the closest hospital on his phone, and once they got Dean into the car, headed there. As DA, Chris was able to get him right in, citing a need to collect evidence for potential criminal charges. He went back with Dean, while Alex sat in the waiting area. Once they were in a room and Dean was on the bed, he looked at Chris.

"Is Alex okay?"

"She was scared to death that something worse happened to you. Tyler isn't who we thought he was, but we'll talk about that later. We need to focus on you now."

A few minutes later, a lab tech walked in to do the blood draw. They would be rushing the results given the urgency of the case. Depending on what Tyler slipped him, they only had a limited time before the drug would be out of his system.

Dean looked at his watch and said, "It hasn't been more than a couple of hours, so I don't understand why Alex was so upset."

"Actually it's been longer. Today's Friday."

Dean went white and looked like he was going to pass out.

"Deep breaths, buddy. You're safe now."

Dean took a couple of breaths like Chris instructed and he started to calm down. About an hour later, a doctor entered his room.

"I'm Dr. Waters. I have the results of Mr. Fox's bloodwork. Mr. Fox, do I have permission to speak in front of your guest?"

"Yes."

"Very well. We found a large amount of Rohypnol in your system. You're lucky that nothing worse happened to you. I have a report prepared with our findings. Do you have any idea how you came to ingest the drug?"

Dean looked at Chris.

"Doctor, we believe Mr. Fox was drugged, which is why we brought him in. We know who allegedly committed the act, so I will need a copy of the report for my case."

"Of course, provided that Mr. Fox agrees. Otherwise, I'll need a warrant."

"Understood."

Dean responded, "I consent."

"Okay, I'll have the nurse bring a form for you to sign. Unless you think there's a reason, I don't feel we need to admit the patient, provided he won't be going home alone tonight.

"You have my word, doctor."

"Okay, please sit tight until the nurse returns with the consent form and discharge papers."

While they were waiting, Chris ran out to the waiting area and handed his keys and valet ticket to Alex.

"We'll be heading out shortly. Can you have them bring my car up, so Dean doesn't have to wait?"

"Of course."

Chris returned to Dean's room just as he was signing the papers. They got him loaded into a wheelchair and headed outside. Dean smiled when he saw Alex standing there.

"I took care of paying and tipping the valet, so we can head out."

They got Dean into the front seat with Chris, while Alex climbed in back, and they started the drive back to Lancaster.

"The doctor said I can't be alone tonight."

"I know. You're welcome to stay with me. I have to warn you, though, it can get pretty chaotic with the girls."

A quiet voice from the back said, "He can stay with me."

Chris saw his friend's face light up like a Christmas tree and he knew that was exactly where Dean needed to be. When they arrived at Alex's house, Chris helped her get him inside and over to the couch.

"I'm going to head out and get some sleep, but I'll be back later to check on you."

Alex answered, "Thanks for everything, Chris."

Dean nodded as he let out a huge yawn. Chris waved and headed out, and Alex locked the door behind him.

Chapter Eight

"Can I get you anything, or do you just want to sleep?"

"I wanna talk more, but I need to sleep. Could you get me a blanket?"

"Why do you need a blanket?"

"So I can lay down and go to sleep."

"You don't think for one second you're sleeping on this couch do you?"

"I did."

"No way. Follow me to my bedroom. You deserve a nice comfy bed to sleep in."

"Are you sure?"

"Yes. My couch pulls out, so I will sleep here."

"Thank you."

After she got Dean settled, she closed her bedroom door, and got the couch setup. She quickly fell asleep, but was awakened a couple hours later by screaming.

"Stop, please, don't."

She quietly opened her bedroom door and saw Dean thrashing around, clearly having a nightmare. She didn't want to startle him by waking him, so she sat down in the chair on the other side of the room.

He awakened a little while later, again looking confused until he saw her sitting there.

"What are you doing in here?"

"You were having a nightmare, so I didn't want to leave you alone."

"I'm sorry."

"For what?"

"Being so much trouble."

"Stop that. I'm the one who needs to apologize."

"Why are you sorry?"

"If it wasn't for me, you wouldn't have been drugged."

"You didn't do it, Tyler did."

"But if I hadn't become friends with him."

"Stop. There's no way this was your fault."

"It feels like it was and I'm so sorry."

"The only one to blame is that asshole."

"Thanks, but I will always feel responsible."

Dean heard his stomach growl.

"I haven't eaten since that night at the bar."

"What would you like?"

"If it's no trouble, I could really eat some bacon and scrambled eggs."

"No problem. I love cooking breakfast."

Alex walked out to the kitchen and cooked them both breakfast then carried the plates to the kitchen table. Dean ate his food quickly as he was starving. Any last bit of resistance she had felt toward him was gone. She knew she needed to tell him how she felt, but she was worried about the timing, so she held off. After they were done with breakfast, Alex cleaned up. He tried to help, but she made him rest.

"I really need a shower, but I don't have anything I need here."

"I can drive you home so you can grab some stuff, but you're coming back here with me."

"I've been enough trouble."

"You have not. I l...care about you."

If he heard her almost say love, he didn't let on.

"Thanks."

They headed over to Dean's house so he could pack what he needed. Once he was done, they headed back to Alex's house. Dean walked right to the bathroom so he could shower, while Alex waited in the living room. She looked outside when she heard a car enter her driveway and saw Tyler. She grabbed her cell and ducked into her pantry so Tyler couldn't see her and dialed Chris. She told him Tyler was outside, and that she was scared, especially with Dean still at her house. Chris let her know he was close to her house and would be right there. When he pulled into the driveway, Tyler got spooked and sped off without ever getting out of his car. Chris texted Alex to let her know he was gone so she peeked outside. Once she saw the coast was clear, she opened the door for Chris.

"I was going to call you guys in a bit. I have some news and was just heading off to pick up the last thing I need. The bar agreed to make me a copy of the tape showing Tyler drugging Dean's beer. I spoke to a judge this morning and I have enough to arrest Tyler. I have the warrant and just need to go grab the tape. Once I have that, troopers are going to arrest him. We just need your help, Alex, if you're comfortable."

"What do you need me to do?"

"Call him and invite him to lunch at the diner on Main. Put the phone on speaker and arrange it for 90 minutes from now."

"Okay."

She dialed Tyler's number and he picked up right away.

"Hi Alex."

"Hey. I was hoping you might join me for lunch this afternoon."

"You don't have plans?"

"No, nothing."

"Sure. Where?"

"I love the diner on Main. I just need to get showered and dressed. Does 90 minutes from now work?"

"Sounds great. I can't wait."

Alex disconnected and sighed with relief.

"You did great. I'm going to head down to the station now and ride with one of the troopers. While you're gone, I will have a member of my security detail outside your house until Tyler is in custody so Dean is protected."

A few minutes later, Dean emerged from Alex's bedroom. He looked much better today.

"What's going on?"

Chris filled him on the plan. He looked down when he heard his phone ping letting him know security was outside. Once he finished letting Dean know what was going to happen, he headed to the station so they could be in position. There would be plain-clothed troopers covering all angles so Alex would be safe. Chris called the restaurant and reserved her an outside table. It was safer that way so troopers could keep better eyes on her. When it was time for her to head out, she glanced at Dean. He looked nervous, but didn't say anything. Security nodded as she got in her car. When she arrived Tyler was not yet there. She approached the seating host who took her to the table Chris had requested.

Tyler arrived about ten minutes later. Alex somehow managed a smile. Their waitress, actually an undercover trooper approached, to take their drink orders. They both ordered waters. Their "waitress" put her order book on the table next to Alex, blocking it with her body so Tyler couldn't see it. She saw the word restroom on there, and stood.

"I'll be right back, I need to use the ladies room."

"Okay."

Once Alex was a safe distance from the table, troopers moved in and grabbed Tyler. They placed him under arrest, cuffed him, and read him his rights. After running through the list of charges, they put him in the back of one of the police cars and sped away. Alex came back out as Chris was approaching.

"You did great. Now get home and take care of my friend."

"Thank you for everything, Chris."

Chris nodded and turned to speak with the troopers still on site. Alex smiled as she walked back to her car to head home. She couldn't get there fast enough, eager to see Dean and tell him this was over. When she got home, Chris's security detail let her know he would be rotating in with other guards for at least a couple of days until they make sure Tyler doesn't get sprung somehow. Alex thanked him and headed inside.

"It's over. I wish you could have seen him cuffed and dragged away."

"Thank god."

Would you like something to eat?"

"I'm starving, so food would be great."

"Any requests?"

"I would love some lunch?"

"Anything you want."

Dean raised his eyebrows, but he didn't answer. She had a feeling she knew what was on his mind.

"I always loved your grilled cheese with bacon sandwich."

"You got it."

After lunch, Dean was getting sleepy, so he went into Alex's bedroom to take a nap. While he was asleep, she got dinner prepared so all she had to do was heat it up when he was ready to eat. A few hours later, he emerged from her bedroom, looking well-rested.

"Something smells good out here."

"I threw together a meatloaf and mashed potatoes. Everything's all cooked so I just have to heat up a couple plates. I also have creamed spinach."

"Delicious," he said as he eyed her up and down.

She prepared two plates and heated them in the microwave then carried them over to the table. It didn't take Dean long to finish, as he was still starving after a couple days of not eating. Alex put the dishes in the sink and returned to the table.

"Are you up for a walk down to the pond?"

"Love to."

They walked outside and Alex told security where they were headed. They walked down and sat on the small dock, right next to each other. Having her that close took his breath away. Damn, he loved that woman.

"Are you up for talking now?"

"Yes."

"You really hurt me when you left."

"I know."

"I can't go through that again."

"Me either."

"Good. I need to tell you something then."

"Tell me."

"I still love you and I want to give things another try. I can't stand the thought of spending another night not in your arms. I was already starting to feel this way, and had planned to tell you when we went out to dinner, but then everything else happened."

"Baby, you don't know how long I've waited to hear you say that. I love you. I really want to show you how much."

Dean put a hand under her chin and gently turned her head toward his, kissing her tenderly. His touch awakened something inside her soul, removing any last little doubt she had about giving their love another chance. His touch also awakened her body, especially her most intimate parts. They sat for a while just holding hands, gazing out at the water, before deciding to head back to the house.

"Would you like something for dessert? I have an apple pie in the fridge."

"I'd love a piece."

Of you, he thought to himself.

She cut two pieces and brought them over to the table. As they sat and ate, they gazed at each other lovingly. After they were done, Dean turned some music on and asked her to dance. Wrapped in each other's arms, they swayed slowly in the middle of her living room, as they kissed passionately. After a couple of songs, Dean asked her for something to drink.

"What would you like?"

"Iced tea."

"Coming right up."

So's my dick, he thought to himself. Damn he wanted her. He was hoping she would have been his dessert. He sat at the table just staring at her hot ass while she poured two glasses of iced tea. Once the sandwiches were ready, she brought them to the table along with two glasses of iced tea. They sat down and drank, never taking their eyes off each other. When they were done, Alex cleared the table and cleaned up all the dishes.

"Can I get you anything else right now?"

Dean didn't utter a word. Instead, he walked over, and pulled Alex tight against him, as if he was holding on for dear life. He kissed her with more intensity than she'd ever felt from him, his tongue eagerly exploring her mouth. She had never wanted a man more than she wanted him at that moment. She took his hand and walked him to her bedroom.

Chapter Nine

"Alex..."

"Sssh."

Alex wrapped her arms around Dean, looked up and kissed him as passionately as he had in her living room. She felt Dean's strong hands slip under shirt and rub her back, sending chills through her entire body. She took her hands and moved them to his chest, lifting his shirt off. He was still just as sexy as she remembered. Her shirt and bra quickly hit the floor, and they embraced again, loving the feeling of being skin on skin. The rest of their clothes came off and they laid down together on Alex's bed.

Laying on their sides facing each other, they gazed into each others' eyes, their hearts filled with more love then either knew was possible. Unable to resist her for one more second, Dean laid her on her back and lowered his head, sucking gently on her breasts, teasing her nipples with his tongue. He slid his tongue down to her belly and showered her with soft kisses, making her shiver with pleasure. She ran her hands all over his sexy chest. He let out a deep groan as he felt her tongue caressing his sexy chest and abs.

"Damn, baby, that feels so good. Now relax your body while I work my magic on you."

Alex's pussy was wet with anticipation, allowing Dean's skillful fingers to slide inside her with ease. He moved his fingers in and out slowly while he massaged her clit with his thumb.

"Oh, that feels amazing."

"Just wait, baby, I have a lot more pleasure in store for you. I really want to taste you baby."

Before Alex could respond, Dean slid down her body, and slowly caressed her beautiful pussy with his tongue. Alex arched her back as she moaned in pleasure, her fingers running through his gorgeous hair.

"Mmmm, oh Dean, oh god. I've missed you so much. Oh god, please don't stop, mmm. Ohhhhh, Dean."

Dean continued pleasuring her with his tongue until her entire body started shaking.

"Holy shit, so fucking good, mmmm, oh, Dean," she screamed in ecstasy.

Dean was about to speak when Alex stopped him.

"That was incredible. Get on your back now."

"My, my, aren't we eager?"

Alex didn't answer, and instead used her mouth for something else. She moved her head down and wrapped her lips around Dean's massive cock. He groaned with pleasure as she slid her lips and tongue up and down his rock-hard shaft.

"Baby, that feels incredible. Damn, I had forgotten how amazing being with you felt."

"I wanna feel you inside me."

Dean gently laid Alex on her back, and smiled as she spread her long, sexy legs for him. He moved on top of her, and slowly slid his dick inside her hot, wet pussy. Alex released a long sigh, clearly indicating her pleasure. It was the most beautiful sound he'd ever heard. He continued slowly and passionately sliding his dick in and out of her.

Alex wrapped her arms around him and rubbed his back with her beautiful hands. He leaned down and kissed her as they continued their passionate lovemaking. Dean's slow and deliberate thrusting made this last for over an hour and when they finally reached that beautiful climax together, they were both screaming in ecstasy. They kissed as they rode wave after wave of their incredible orgasms, both of their bodies quivering from head to toe.

Dean laid down next to his beautiful woman and pulled her close, again kissing her with passion. She reached her hands out to start touching him, her body aching to feel him inside her again.

"Not so fast, baby."

She loved that he took charge. With the farm, she was always the boss, so she liked having someone else take the reins. She waited for instructions. Dean was also enjoying this. After being under the thumb of the record company for so many years, he liked the freedom that came with telling someone else what to do. As long as Alex was willing, he would keep going.

"I want you."

"I want you too."

"Tell me what to do."

"Baby, come straddle me and wrap that pretty mouth around my cock."

Alex climbed on top of her sexy lover and lowered her head, taking his massive dick in her mouth. She slid her lips and tongue up and down slowly, teasing him.

Dean growled loudly, "Fuck, that feels so damn good. But now I really need to feel your pussy around my dick. Baby, slide up here and take me inside you."

Alex smiled as she slid up his body and lowered herself onto his huge dick, taking him deep inside her. She moaned loudly at the intense pleasure.

"That's right, baby, let me hear you. "

As Alex bounced up and down on Dean, he matched her with powerful thrusts, adding even more pleasure until Alex lost all control.

She cried out, "Oh, Dean, nobody ever made me feel as fucking incredible as you. Oh, fuck, so good Dean. Harder, oh god, Dean."

Alex could feel herself close to climaxing and started to increase her speed.

"No, baby, go slow."

Alex slowed down as the pressure kept building. When she finally reached the point of ultimate release, her entire body was on fire. She felt pleasure inside her pussy like nothing she'd ever experienced, even in their past encounters. She screamed loudly as her pussy exploded in the most powerful orgasm she'd ever had. Her reaction got Dean so hot that he quickly shot his load inside her. She slid off him and laid next to him, her chest heaving from the intensity of their fucking.

"Oh, Dean, there are not enough words to describe how that felt. My entire body is tingling."

"Alexandra, I hope you're not tired yet."

"Not at all. I'm completely exhilarated from what you just did to me."

"Well then we better get moving, babe."

They spent the next several hours holding each other close, passionately loving each other. Each kiss, each thrust, each incredible orgasm made Alex feel more and more love, as every last brick of the wall around her heart crumbled away. When they were both completely drained of energy, Dean laid next to her and held her in his arms. He pulled her close and kissed her tenderly then pulled the covers over their naked bodies. They quickly drifted off to sleep, wrapped in each other's arms.

While they were napping, Chris stopped by to see how they were doing. The security detail he had covering Alex's house stopped him from going in.

"I assure you they're doing just fine. I think they may be sleeping right now."

"Are you sure they're okay?"

"Oh, yeah," he said with a smirk.

"Spill it."

"All the windows are wide open and let's just say they aren't quiet."

"Ah, got it. I'll call later."

Chris smiled as he returned to his car, happy that his friend had made his way back to the woman of his dreams. He would wait until tomorrow to tell them what they found out about Tyler. It was bone-chilling to say the least.

They awakened a couple hours later, completed famished.

"What would you like for dinner?"

"I want to take you out."

"Are you sure after what you've been through?"

Looking down at their naked bodies, he smiled and said, "Clearly, I'm good."

She returned his smile and said, "Okay. Let's go."

"One minor problem."

"What?"

"I don't have another change of clothes."

"If you give me a key, I'll run over to you house and get what you need. Then when I get back we can shower and head out."

"Under one condition."

"What?"

"Well, given my ordeal, I don't think showering alone is a good idea," he said with a naughty wink.

"Well, far be it from me not to help my man get clean since I helped get him dirty."

He handed his keys to Alex and let her know what he needed and where to find everything. She returned with a bag about 20 minutes later. Dean was still in bed, Holly laying there with him, in heaven as she was getting belly rubs from him.

"I leave for twenty minutes and I get replaced. I thought I was your only woman."

Dean laughed out loud and got out of bed. He walked over and grabbed Alex, pulling her close. Before she knew what was happening, he had her naked. Still the same sexy man she fell for all those years ago. They walked together to her bathroom and got in the shower. They held each other tight as the hot water cascaded down their bodies. Alex grabbed Dean's shower gel and a washcloth. She breathed deep, inhaling the scent of his sexy gel, drooling from her mouth and between her legs. He returned the favor, thoroughly enjoying the flowery scent of her gel. After very sensually washing each other, they got out and dried off, then headed back to Alex's bedroom to get dressed.

"After dinner, I want to stop back at my house and grab more clothes, if you'll allow me to spend the rest of the weekend here."

"You better. I have a feeling you're going to need to spend quite a bit of time in bed this weekend."

"But I'm really not tired. I feel fine."

"I didn't say we would be in bed to sleep."

"Damn, woman!"

They headed to Alex's favorite buffet for dinner. They ended up spending a couple of hours sitting and talking, realizing there was a lot about each other they needed to get reacquainted with. Alex loved hearing some of Dean's stories about life on the road and the definite up and downs of the music business. Despite in her mind how much more interesting his stories were, Dean paid as close attention to her as she had him. He loved hearing the way she talked about her friends and all the fun they have together. He did find himself wishing he had been here for her during the loss of her father, but he couldn't change the past. All he could do now was make sure he was here for her going forward.

After they finished eating, they headed out to Alex's car.

"How about a walk around the park before we head back to my house?"

"Sounds good."

Alex drove to their local park, one of her favorite places when she needed a break from life. Holding hands the whole time, they circled the walking track a few times before stopping for a break at one of the benches. Dean put an arm around Alex as she rested her head on his shoulder. It was easily the most content he'd ever felt and he was so thankful he made the decision to move back here. Of course, the closeness of her warm body was also evoking other feelings as well, threatening to cause a stirring in his jeans. He smiled wide as he remembered the fun they had in her bed earlier. Turns out, he wasn't the only one feeling something in his jeans, as the longer Alex sat with him, the wetter she got until she could barely stand it.

"Um, I think we need to go home. Now!"

'Yeah. Right now!"

Like two horny teenagers, they practically ran back to her car and sped home. They raced into the house to the amusement of the security guard out front and straight to Alex's bedroom. Clothes were flying everywhere as they eagerly stripped each other naked and laid down in bed. Alex got on her hands and knees, lowered her head and wrapped her lips around his massive cock. She slid her mouth and tongue up and down his shaft until he could no longer take it.

"Baby, I'm about to explode."

Alex licked him harder and faster until she felt his hot cream fill her mouth. She lifted her head and swallowed every last drop then teasingly licked her lips making his dick hard again. Dean sat up, wrapped his arms around his goddess and rolled her onto her back. He ran his hands all over her skin, setting her body on fire. He gently spread her legs, and slid two fingers inside her, stroking her g-spot hard, as she writhed in pleasure.

"Oh, Dean, that feels amazing."

Dean kept up the pressure, as her moaning became louder and louder. Her entire body was quaking as she exploded into the most intense orgasm Dean had ever seen a woman have, as she drenched his hand.

"Babe, that was the sexiest fucking thing I've ever seen. You're so damn hot, and I need to have my dick inside you NOW."

"Come fuck me hard, you sexy beast."

He climbed on top of her, and slid his dick inside her, thrusting hard. Her pussy was still soaking wet from her incredible orgasm, feeling even hotter wrapped around Dean's cock. He thrust in and out of her with loving passion, until he exploded inside her. He laid down next to her and pulled her close, both of them drenched in sweat and other delicious fluids from their incredible sex. He kissed her hard, sliding his tongue into her mouth. She met his kiss with equal passion, as their kissing matched the intensity of their lovemaking. When they finally came up for air, Dean spoke quietly.

"Alexandra, I need to tell you something and please know, I'm not trying to scare you. Baby, you're unlike any woman I've ever known and I never stopped being completely in love with you. I love you and I don't want to know one more moment of my life without you in it. I'm in this for the long haul."

"I never thought I would hear a man say that to me after you left. And I'm definitely still in love with you too. I love you so much. The only thing that does scare me is losing you."

They spent the rest of the night in each others' arms, making love until they were both so spent, they fell asleep still holding each other.

Chapter Ten

Dean and Alex woke up around noon, completely refreshed from a deep sleep. They got up and showered together then went downstairs for some breakfast. After they finished eating they cleaned up. Dean walked over and sat on her couch, so she joined him, planting herself in his lap. He wrapped his arms around her waist and held her close.

Gazing lovingly into his gorgeous blue eyes, she asked, "Anything you want to do today?"

"I would love to see how you do things around here. You seem to be so well known and respected at the market, which I love."

They headed out the back door to where Alex had her hen house and the storage for all her harvested crops. Dean held her hand as they walked over. Even that innocent of a touch from this man was spreading heat through her whole body, especially in her panties. Once they were inside, Dean couldn't believe how massive the storage was.

"Wow, this is bigger than I would have ever guessed."

Like something else, she thought naughtily to herself.

"And you run this all by yourself?"

"I'm the owner and boss, yes, but no I definitely do not run this by myself. My father was a firm believer that you are nothing without your employees and he treated them exactly that way. Even though I changed farms when he passed away, I kept the same staff. Very rarely do we have to hire here. The only time we've ever had anyone leave is for retirement. I have not changed one thing that he put in place for the employees since I took over."

"After what I dealt with working for that record company, hearing that there are people like you now and your dad before you is very refreshing. I'm sure he's looking down at you with so much pride."

"Thank you so much. My dad adored you, even after you left. He helped me understand about your dream and why you left. I wish he was still here. Fucking cancer."

Dean saw a couple of tears spilled out of her eyes. He wrapped her in his arms and kissed her tenderly on the head. After a few minutes, she had regained her composure.

"How about that tour now?"

"Let's do it, my sexy tour guide."

Alex walked him around the the rest of farm, showing him the stables, the staff quarters and the break area she built for her employees.

"Wow, this is incredible. No wonder employees never leave."

"My dad always believed that a relaxed employee was a more efficient employee. The state has laws for minimum break times allowed, but my dad always doubled those times and they were always paid. We've always provided full insurance coverage for our employees and their families and we are also generous with our vacation and other time away from work. It has always paid dividends as our staff works harder than most people because they are so appreciated."

"I love hearing you talk this much about your dad, and I would definitely love to learn more about him."

Alex smiled as images of her dad floated through her head. She took Dean down to where there was a garage, showing him a fleet if golf carts.

"Dad bought those when some of his longtime staff started getting older and couldn't do as much walking. He just cared so much about people. Why did that fucking disease have to steal him from all of us?"

Dean put a hand on her arm to comfort her, as they walked more of the property. Dean walked over to a large privacy fence and peeked inside. He noticed there was a big swimming pool with a small hot tub attached. He would love to be to spend more time down here.

The view was stunning, though not as stunning as the woman he was with.

They went into the pool area and sat down on the bench she had in there. Dean put his arm around her.

"Oh, baby, we could have some fun right here."

"Mmm, I can only imagine."

Alex started picturing being naked in the pool with him and felt that familiar heat spreading between her legs. Suddenly feeling bold, she got up, took her clothes off and climbed into the pool. Dean just sat there, his mouth hanging open at the site of his naked goddess in the water. Once he recovered, he stripped down and joined her, wrapping her in his arms. She kissed him hard, sliding her tongue in his mouth with an eagerness. Dean started sucking on her neck as Alex ran her fingers through his gorgeous dark hair. She loved feeling his naked body against hers. He pulled away and swam over to the edge of pool. After climbing out, he sat in the grass next to the pool, as she joined him.

"Dean, I would love to fuck you like this."

"Oh my, you sure are feeling naughty today. Please, baby, sit on my cock. I want you so damn bad, I'm aching with desire."

Alex sat down on his lap, taking his dick inside of her pussy. He wrapped his arms around as she bounced up and down on his cock.

"Fuck, baby, you feel so good wrapped around my cock."

"Oh, Dean, it's so good, oh god, baby. I love how incredible your dick feels inside me. I love the feeling of feeling your skin against mine."

Dean watched with a huge smile on his as her ample breasts bounced as she continued riding him hard. Dean could feel her breathing increase as she moved closer and closer to climax.

"Oh, Dean, oh fuck. Sooo fucking good."

While her body quaked with a powerful orgasm, she kissed Dean passionately as she kept riding him until she felt him shoot a load of hot cum inside her. She collapsed against his body as he held her tight.

"Baby, that was amazing. You're such an incredible lover, baby."

"I love spending time at my pool, but this is by far the most fun I've had here. I love you."

"Alexandra, I love you too, my sexy angel."

They got dressed and headed back to the house. Just as they had reached the back door, they heard a car come up the driveway and saw Chris parking in front of the house. Dean called to him as he and Alex headed to her driveway. Chris smiled when he saw that they were soaking wet.

"And just where you two?"

"Took a quick dip in my pool."

Chris smiled and raised his eyebrows but didn't say a word. Instead he walked toward her front porch.

"Can we go inside and talk? I have some new information regarding Tyler."

Dean and Alex nodded and they all headed into her house. Dean and Alex sat on the couch and Chris stood, pacing the floor.

"I don't even know where to begin, but I think I'll start with the good news. The bail hearing is set for tomorrow morning and with what my investigation turned up, he is almost guaranteed to be denied bail."

Alex and Dean both breathed a sigh of relief.

"Now for the troubling information. First, let me say, Dean, you're lucky. You may not think so, but Tyler made a mistake in your case. He forgot to take your wallet. He's done this several times before in different states. In the past cases I could find, he always took the wallet along with the phone to further delay the ID of his victim."

He took a break as he saw Dean shudder. He was wishing that was all he had to tell him. This last part was really going to upset Alex, but he needed them to know everything.

"There's one more thing you need to know. We finished reviewing the internal GPS from his phone and we found a set of coordinates where he spent an exceptionally large amount of time recently. We thought it was likely his home given how many hours were tracked, but when we followed the coordinates, we found a spot close to her where your house is completely visible, Alex."

"So, he-he-he was watching me?"

"I'm so sorry, but I needed you to be prepared for anything you might hear. Even though he's locked up and likely not getting out, we're going to keep security in place for now."

Chris saw Dean pull Alex a little tighter against him. He was glad they made their way back to each other. Hoping to lighten the mood, he had one more tidbit for them.

"Oh, one other thing, not related to Tyler, and I only tell you this in hopes of lightening the mood a bit, if that's okay."

"We could use it," Alex said.

"You might want to close your windows during, um, certain activities. My security detail got quite the audio treat."

They all laughed, Alex also turning a deep shade of red.

"I'll be at the hearing tomorrow as the DA, so I will let you know once everything is settled."

They thanked Chris for all his help, as they walked him to his car. Alex couldn't bring herself to even look in the direction of the guard after what Chris told them, which had Dean and Chris doubled over in laughter. It was a much-needed distraction from everything Chris had told them. They headed back inside and sat down for a moment to let everything sink in. After a few minutes of just sitting and holding each other, Dean's stomach started growling.

"Hmmm, must have been our workout at the pool," Alex said, smiling.

"Okay, my naughty girl. How about some lunch? I have a serious craving for some pizza and I figure you probably know the best places."

"Sounds good. I have a favorite place, especially if you like pepperoni. Angelo's has been in business since I was kid. Every Friday, my dad would take me there for dinner, so it holds a special place in my heart. My dad was friends with Angelo himself, so he will never let me pay when I go in. I always sneak some extra money in his tip jar when he's not looking."

"That's so awesome. I love learning all these new things about you. After so many years of dealing with so many phony people, I love that I've been able to come back to someone so real."

Alex smiled as she got in her car. Once Dean was in, she headed to Angelo's. She parked in front of the restaurant and went inside. When Angelo saw her, he came over and gave her a big hug.

In a thick Italian accent, Angelo asked, "And who might this be, Miss Alex?"

With a bright smile on her face, she answered, "This is my

boyfriend, Dean. He just moved into the farm next to mine a few weeks ago."

Angelo gave Dean a hug. "Any friend of Alex's is always welcome here. This young lady is like a daughter to me. Come, let me take you to your special table. Shall I bring your usual?"

"Yes, please, just in a large this time. Thank you, Angelo."

"Anything for you," Angelo said warmly.

He headed to the kitchen to prepare their pizza himself. While they waited, Dean held Alex's hands across the table. He loved this woman more than he ever knew was possible. A little while later, Angelo approached their table with their pizza along with a bottle of wine and two glasses. He smiled broadly when he saw them holding hands.

"Your pizza, my friends, and a bottle of wine on the house to celebrate your new love."

He poured them each a glass and left the bottle on the table.

"Angelo, thank you so much. You are sweet." Alex got up and kissed Angelo on the cheek then sat back down. Angelo shook Dean's hand and told them both to enjoy their meal, then headed back to the kitchen. Dean and Alex never stopped gazing into each others' eyes as they ate. Alex had never known this kind of love and it felt amazing.

When they finished eating, Dean asked for the check, but Angelo refused. He and Alex hugged Angelo goodbye, dropped some money in the tip jar and headed out to Alex's car.

"I am seeing more and more how important your dad was to the town, Alex."

"He truly was. He was kind, fair, and generous. I know getting sick isn't indicative of how he lived, but he was definitely the last person that deserved cancer."

"I wish there was something I could say. That disease just fucking sucks, but just think how proud you're making your father. I hope that brings you some comfort, my angel."

"Thank you. I love you."

"Baby, I love you too. How about we go home and I show you how much?"

"I would love to, but I need to get everything ready for the market. Would you be okay waiting until after I get done and get a shower?"

"Under one condition, babe."

"I'm afraid to ask, but what condition?"

"That you let me come help you. We will get done faster together."

"Dean, I didn't get back together with you so you will do work for me."

"I know, baby. I just want to spend every possible moment I can with you, and that includes helping you at the farm."

Alex sighed, knowing she didn't have a prayer of winning this argument.

"Okay, you stubborn dickhead."

Dean laughed and lightly swatted her on her hot ass.

"Mmmm, I kinda liked that. Maybe we can do more of that later."

"You mean, you would let me spank you?"

"Mmmm, yes please. The thought of your hands on my ass excites me. I'm definitely getting wet, baby."

Dean felt his dick starting to get hard and had to fight to calm himself. They were back in her driveway, so Alex parked and they headed to the storage area.

"Okay, boss lady, I am awaiting my assignment."

"I like the idea of bossing you around a bit, Dean. Watch out or I may want to do that in the bedroom one night."

Dean walked over to Alex and nuzzled her neck.

"Anytime you want, my sexy tigress."

Alex turned her head and kissed Dean passionately. He felt her tongue eagerly exploring his mouth.

"Baby, if you keep that up, you're going to wake the snake."

"My office. Now!"

Alex turned and headed toward the back, Dean in tow. They went into her office and Alex locked the door behind them.

"Dean I want to ride you right there on my couch."

They quickly and eagerly removed their clothes. Dean sat down on the couch. Alex sat, facing him and took his dick deep inside her. She moaned loudly as she slid up and down his massive cock, his hands on her hips for support.

"Baby, I love watching your beautiful breasts bouncing in my face. Fuck, you're so incredible."

Alex rode her cowboy harder and harder until her entire body was shaking with an earth-shattering orgasm. She screamed in ecstasy as wave after wave of pleasure coursed through her veins. Watching her enjoy this so much, and feeling her pussy tighten around him as she came sent Dean over the edge. He groaned loudly as he filled her with his hot cum. Alex collapsed against his sexy chest, both of them breathing heavy after their fast and furious sex.

"So much for waiting, huh, baby?"

"I find it impossible to resist that sexy, muscular body. Mmmm, so hot."

Alex kissed him then climbed off and started getting dressed.

"Time to get to work, chop chop."

"Oh, so you have your way with me then it's back to work. I see how things are."

Dean laughed as Alex tried to look annoyed but she couldn't find it and she doubled over in laughter.

"Seriously, though, I guess we should get moving since we got a little sidetracked there."

"I need to get everything boxed and weighed so I can keep track of my inventory."

"I'm happy to get everything boxed while you weigh them since I don't know your process."

"Works for me. Thank you so much, and I don't mean for helping me box up everything," she said as she gave a smack on his sexy bottom.

Grinning from ear to ear, Dean followed her to where she kept empty boxes and helped her carry a couple stacks out to the table. Dean filled the boxes as Alex weighed everything and entered the information into her laptop. It took them a couple of hours. It would have normally taken Alex twice that and she was grateful for the help. Once they were done, they had dinner and spent the rest of the evening hanging on the couch binge watching Alex's favorite show until they could no longer keep their eyes open. They headed to bed and fell asleep holding each other tight.

Chapter Eleven

Alex awoke the next morning and found herself alone in bed. She picked up the delicious scent of coffee and bacon causing her stomach to start growling. She got up and went to the kitchen only to see Dean standing there cooking in nothing but an apron and a cowboy hat. She licked her lips when she saw his sexy naked ass.

"Woo hoo, look at that sexy cowboy."

She walked over to him and ran her hands over his butt, causing him to groan in pleasure.

"Good morning, my sexy tigress. I thought you might be hungry this morning."

"I am but not for what's in that pan. I want to taste what's under that apron."

"In due time, my angel. But first, we must fuel our bodies for what I promise will be a fun morning."

Hearing his words sent that familiar heat between her legs as her breathing became more rapid in anticipation of the pleasure he would bring her.

"Would you mind pouring the coffee while I finish up the eggs?"

"Not at all, sexy."

Alex poured them each a cup of coffee and sat down at the table.

Dean carried over two plates of delicious looking food. Not as delicious as him, she thought to herself. Damn, this man was hot. Her lips curled up in a naughty smile as she saw him sitting there. She imagined ripping that apron off him and pressing her naked body against his.

"Mmm, this tastes so good, baby," she said in a voice so sultry that Dean almost fell off his chair, as he felt his dick starting to stir.

After they finished eating, Dean said, "Babe, we can clean up later. I can't wait one more minute to take you back to bed."

He stood up and removed his apron. Alex looked him up and down, making love to him with her eyes, as she noticed his dick was rock hard. She was going to be late arriving at the market but she didn't care.

Putting a stern look on her face, she commanded, "Bedroom. Now."

"Yes ma'am," Dean responded as he practically ran down the hall.

When they were back in her bedroom, Alex continued her instructions.

"Come undress me, Slowly. And I better be pleased by your performance."

Dean smiled, loving this side of her. He walked over to her, slowly lifting her shirt, his fingers caressing her skin. She felt shivers through her entire body. He ran his hands along her soft shoulders then down to her breasts, gently massaging them as he kissed her neck. She breathed deeply, taking in the sexy musk of his aftershave mixed with his desire for her body. This man was truly intoxicating, and she loved the drunken feeling he brought to her.

Dean got down on his knees and slid her shorts and panties down to her ankles. He showered her stomach with kisses as she felt his strong hands caressing her naked ass. Barely able to contain herself, she ordered him to his feet. Alex laid down on the bed and spread her legs wide.

"What can I do next to please you, my love?" Dean asked.

"I want you to lick and suck my pussy until I explode, baby."

Dean walked over to the bed, knelt down, and licked her pussy up and down, stopping to suck on her clit. Alex writhed and moaned in ecstasy as Dean licked and sucked her slowly, bringing her closer and closer to that magical apex.

Her entire body was shaking as she screamed out, "Oh fuck, Dean, baby, don't stop. So good, oh baby. You may rise now."

Dean stood up, smiling, loving this side of her. Alex looked him up and down with the naughtiest look he'd ever seen on a woman's face.

"You've been a very good lover so far. Tigress is pleased. Now, baby, bring that massive cock over her and fuck my hot, wet pussy."

Dean just about shot his load right on the spot, hearing her sexy commands. He climbed onto the bed and lowered himself onto his precious love, sliding his dick inside her.

"I want you deeper, baby."

Dean slid his hands under her ass and lifted her hips off the bed, then entered her again.

"Does that please you, my love?"

"Oh, yes. Your dick feels incredible. Please go slow. I want this to last."

Dean slowed down his thrusts, growling at how incredible it felt being inside her. They moved together slowly and passionately, their breathing in perfect sync, as they truly became one. One heart, one body, one soul, joined in the ecstasy of passionate lovemaking. Alex wrapped her arms around her lover, massaging his muscular ass, trying to take him in even deeper. When they finally reached that ultimate pinnacle together, they moaned and sighed as their bodies experienced wave after wave of perfect pleasure.

"I love you, Alexandra."

"I love you, Dean."

Dean laid down next to her and pulled her close. Chests heaving, bodies drenched in sweat, they kissed each other passionately, tongues dancing, basking in the afterglow of incredible sex.

"Baby, how would you like to get away for a couple of days? I would love to take you to the Poconos this weekend. I know of a resort there that is for couples only. They have a variety of packages you can order. If you're comfortable, I would like to try something a little naughtier than what we've done so far."

"As long as you promise there won't be any pain, I am willing to be a little daring. I could use a couple of days away."

"Baby, I promise no pain. There will be toys, but only those that bring pleasure and, only if you are truly willing, tying your wrists and putting a blindfold on you."

"The thought of all that excites me, but only if I get to tie you up too."

Dean let out an animal-like growl. Just the thought of being tied up by his beautiful tigress was threatening to send his rocket into orbit.

"Oh, baby, I would love to have you tie me up and have your way with me. I may have already made the reservation. Can you leave the market at lunchtime on Friday?"

"Of course. Speaking of the market, though, I really need to get packed and get down there."

"Well, then, let's grab a quick shower and go."

"You don't need to help me."

"I want to."

"Okay," she said smiling.

They drove her car down to the storage area so they could load the boxes for today then headed off to the market. Dean helped her carry everything in. She had to admit, she loved watching those muscles work and she had to fight hard to contain herself. Alex couldn't help but wonder what would happen with Tyler's booth. No time to focus on that now though as she was flooded with customers and was so grateful to have Dean here helping.

Things finally slowed around mid-afternoon. Alex and Dean were taking a much-needed rest and enjoying a quick lunch when Chris stopped by.

"Hey guys. I come bearing some good news. Tyler was denied bail so he's not getting out. His trial is scheduled to start in about two weeks."

He reached into his pocket, pulled out a phone and handed it to Dean.

"Your phone has been released from evidence."

"Thank you both for the phone and for making sure that asshole stays locked up."

Alex added, "I know this is going to sound strange, but what will happen with Daisy? I just want to make sure she's taken care of."

"My girls fell in love with her at the picnic, so the court agreed to award me ownership."

Alex smiled, happy that his dog wouldn't suffer because of the actions of her former owner.

"I'm waiting for the local sheriff now so we can go close down his booth. The assets will all be seized and put towards the cost of his trial. The booth will now be available for another tenant."

"I know just the person to take that over. My friend Hannah owns a kickass pet supply store. She could rent this booth out and have another place to sell her inventory. I'm gonna go give her a call."

Dean and Chris talked while Alex went in the back to call Hannah.

"So, things are good with Alex?"

"Yeah. She's amazing."

"Glad to see you so happy, my friend."

"I owe a lot of it to you."

"Fuck yeah you do!"

"Do we have anything to worry about with Tyler?"

"Not anymore. We can put that behind us. I won't need you or Alex in court, so you can focus on her."

"Thank you for everything."

"You got it man. I just saw the sheriff, so I gotta go. Have fun," he said, giving Dean a friendly punch on the arm.

Alex came back out a few minutes after Chris left.

"Chris have to leave?"

"Yeah, sherriff arrived, so he want over to Tyler's booth with him"

"Got it. Hannah is going to call, as she would love to take over that space."

"Cool."

"I'll have to take you to her store sometime. I get all of Holly's stuff there, as well as some things for my horse."

"I'd love to see it."

Alex smiled and reached up to kiss him. She never got tired of feeling any kind of touch with him, though there were some she enjoyed a lot more than others! Wait until we get home later. Just the thought of being naked with him excited her in the most intimate of places. Business picked up again as they approached closing time, so the rest of the day flew by. Once they packed up, they headed back to Alex's house. She was glad to see the security detail was now gone. She was grateful they had them until they knew they were safe, but she definitely felt better now.

"How about we change things up tonight?"

"What'd you have in mind?"

"I want you and Holly spend the night at my house."

"I'd love the change in scenery. Just need to get a few things packed then we can head over."

They went inside and Dean waited while Alex grabbed what she needed for herself and Holly then they headed over to Dean's house. Alex realized this would be the first time she'd seen the place since Dean bought it and she was excited to see what he had done with it. Mostly, though, she wanted to see the bedroom. He took her on a tour and she fell in love with the place, especially the soaking tub in his bathroom. She hoped she got a chance to spend some time in there.

"The place looks great, especially that tub," Alex told him after the tour.

"We could have some fun there."

"Oh yeah we sure could."

"For now, though, how about some dinner?"

"I'm starving."

Dean went to his kitchen to see what he could whip up from the fridge. He found some leftover chicken so he put together two plates of chicken Caesar salad and brought them to the table along with two glasses of wine. After they finished dinner, Alex helped Dean cleanup. When they were done, he pinned Alex against the counter, wrapping her tight in his arms and kissing her passionately, his tongue eagerly exploring her mouth.

"How about we get naked and hit the tub?"

"Mmmm, sounds heavenly."

Alex was so eager to sit naked in the tub with her sexy man that she left a trail of clothes and was completely naked by the time they reached the bathroom. Dean let out a whistle when he saw his sexy naked goddess. He turned on the water and filled the tub. While he was waiting, he undressed, walked over to Alex and pulled her close.

"My sexy tigress."

"Mmmm," she replied, moving her hands to his sexy ass.

They got in the tub and Dean turned on the jets. The feeling of being in the warm water, with the jets massaging her body plus being next to her sexy man, she quickly felt horny as hell and reached her hand under the water.

"Oh, baby."

"I wanna sit on that hard cock."

"Climb on, babe."

Alex moved into her sexy man's lap, facing him, and lowered herself on his hard cock. Fuck, he felt so good that deep inside her. He pulled her chest against his while she slid her pussy up and down his cock, fast and hard until their bodies were surfing waves of incredible pleasure, water splashing everywhere. She kissed him hard, then moved next to him. They both took a little nap as the jets massaged their muscles. They awoke a little while later, dried off and got into their jammies then headed to the living room to snuggle on his couch and watch some TV. When they couldn't keep their eyes open any longer, they headed off to bed.

The rest of the week, luckily, flew by since Alex was so busy. Friday rolled around and all she could think about was their weekend away. Once it hit close to noon, Alex closed down the stand and packed everything up, then headed home to drop off her leftover crops and get packed. Hannah had agreed to watch Holly while she was gone, so she she packed up what she would need and dropped her off then headed over to Dean's house so they could head out. He was waiting outside for her when she pulled up and parked. He walked down, helped her load her luggage into his truck then they headed out.

"Just you wait. We're gonna have a good time," Dean said with a naughty smile on his face.

Alex felt her brain threaten to overload as she imagined the pleasure Dean had in store for her. They hit the Northeast Extension to begin their journey to a weekend of hot, dirty, sweaty sex. All Alex could think about was getting there and getting naked with that sexy man sitting next to her. After a couple hours, Alex was starting to get hungry.

"You hungry, Dean?"

"For you, baby."

"Ha ha, that'll be later."

"You're damn right it will."

Chapter Twelve

D ean saw a diner up ahead, so he pulled into the parking lot and they went inside. After they ordered, they held hands across the table, gazing into each others' eyes until their wait-ress brought their meals. After they finished eating, they got back on the road to finish their drive.

Alex's eyes went wide when Dean pulled up at the resort. The cabins were beautiful outside, and she could only imagine what awaited her on the inside. She felt her pussy getting wet, just thinking about what Dean had in store for her. He went inside to check in and get the key to their cabin. Once he returned, he drove to their cabin. The inside was even more beautiful than the outside. The living room was stun-ning with a bearskin rug in front of a fireplace. Dean saw Alex gazing at the fireplace.

"Baby, imagine how incredible it would feel to fuck in front of the fire."

"Oh, Dean. I want you."

She was so overwhelmed and excited, words were escaping her. Alex headed off to take a look at the rest of cabin, with Dean right behind her, hand on her ass.

"I want to see the bedroom, baby."

They walked down the hall until they reached their destination. Dean opened the door and turned on the light. Alex looked around, taking in all the sights. The walls were painted in crimson red, with a beautiful king-sized bed in the middle, complete with black satin sheets. Connected to the bedroom was a bathroom, including a heart-shaped soaking tub and a large walk-in shower stall, both designed for couples to enjoy together.

Dean walked up behind Alex and wrapped his arms around her, kissing her neck.

"Baby, I want your naked body against mine. Let's fuck."

"Mmm, yes Dean. But can we see what they left for us to play with? I want to turn things up a notch, really get naughty."

"You naughty tigress."

"All thanks to you, sexy."

"You deserve nothing but the best. You're a gem that shines like a bright star in the night sky."

"Oh, Dean," Alex said as she wrapped her arms around her lover.

Dean kissed her tenderly, as they embraced passionately.

"I really want you baby. Let's go take a look at our goodie basket."

"I wish I could say I never used these, but I've spent a lot of time alone."

"You'll never be alone again. Do you want to pick one out to try or do you trust me to pick?"

"Surprise me, sexy."

"Okay, baby. Let's get naked, my goddess."

Alex removed her clothes and laid down on the bed. She loved the feeling of the satin sheets against her skin. Dean also removed his clothes. Damn, she never got tired of the sight of his sexy, muscular body. Dean took a vibrator out of the basket and walked over to the bed. He laid down next to Alex.

"Now just relax baby, and enjoy."

Dean turned the vibrator on and touched it to her pussy.

"Holy shit, Dean, that feels so good. Oh, baby."

Alex writhed in pleasure as he turned the speed up to high, keeping the toy pressed to her clit until she cried out, exploding with a powerful orgasm.

"Oh my god, Dean, that felt so fuckin' amazing. What else is in there?"

"There is definitely some other fun stuff, but I think we should save that until tomorrow. Tonight, I just want to make love to you. I love how good it feels when my dick's inside you. I crave you, my beautiful angel."

"Please, baby, please make love to me."

Dean moved on top of Alex, wrapped her in his strong arms and kissed her tenderly as he slid his dick inside her. He felt her sigh deeply as he slid in and out of her.

"Mmmm, Dean, you feel so good. Oh, baby, mmmm, your dick's so big, baby. I love you."

"I love you Alexandra. The feeling of being inside your hot, beautiful pussy is the most amazing thing I've ever felt, and you're the most amazing woman I've ever felt. I love more than anything, my angel."

Keeping his lover in his arms, his dick still inside her, Dean rolled onto his back, pulling Alex on top of him. She sat up straight, taking Dean even deeper inside. The sight of this beautiful woman on top of him, loving him, pleasuring him, sent him over the edge, and he filled Alex full of his warm cream.

"So good," he growled. "Now it's your turn to orgasm, baby."

"That's okay, you did with the toy."

Alex started to climb off, but Dean stopped her.

"Baby, please stay on top of me. I love watching your sexy body while you ride me. Do you feel what's happening?"

"Oh, Dean, you're hard again. Mmmm, you feel so good."

Alex moaned as she resumed sliding up and down his massive cock. Dean watched, his face filled with delight, as she rode him harder and faster, her beautiful breasts bouncing. She screamed in ecstasy as her entire body exploded. Wave after wave of intense pleasure coursed through her body, as she collapsed down onto Dean's sexy chest. He held her tight as she kissed him, sliding her tongue into his mouth. She was drenched in sweat and felt like she needed a shower.

"Dean, I really need a shower. Will you shower with me, my sexy man?"

"I would love to, Alexandra, but first, how about we take a dip in that tub? I noticed a bottle of bubbles, so I thought it would be fun to sit in a bubble bath, holding each other."

"Oh, Dean, that sounds divine."

They walked to the bathroom. Dean poured a capful of bubbles into the tub then turned on the water. Once the tub was filled, he helped Alex in then followed her. They sat, wrapped in each other's arms, kissing passionately. Dean felt his dick getting hard again. This woman affected him like no other.

"Baby, you naughty temptress, I'm hard again."

"I would love to take care of that for you. Would you sit up on the edge of the tub?"

He lifted himself onto the edge of the tub, exposing his erection. Alex flashed him a naughty smile, then lowered her head and took his dick in her mouth. She sucked hard as she dragged her tongue up and down his shaft. Dean growled in pleasure as his beautiful woman sucked on his dick.

"Baby, you're so good at that. I'm so close to exploding baby."

"I wanna drink you."

Alex started sucking on him again, increasing her speed until she felt Dean shoot his load into her mouth. Gazing into his eyes, she swallowed every last drop as she licked her lips.

"Holy fuckin' shit. I'll never get tired of watching you swallow me, my naughty tigress."

Dean climbed back into the tub, feeling completely sated after his beautiful woman gave him yet another hot blow job. They kissed a little more before Dean spoke.

"Baby, I'm starting to get hungry after all that fun. How about we shower, then go grab a snack?"

"That sounds perfect."

Dean got out of the tub first, then helped Alex out. After he drained the tub, they got into the shower. He turned the shower on then wrapped his arms around her as the hot water cascaded down their naked bodies. They washed each others' bodies and hair. Alex loved the feeling of Dean's fingers caressing her scalp. After they both rinsed and dried their bodies and hair, they headed down to the kitchen, still completely naked, to see what snacks were there.

"I was looking at some of the information in the cabin and saw there was a wine and cheese tasting tour. How would you like to do that tomorrow?"

"That sounds fun, Dean. I love a good glass of wine."

After they finished their snacks, they headed to bed, exhausted from their trip. They quickly fell asleep in the luxurious king-sized bed. The next morning, they headed over to the resort restaurant for a light breakfast then a walk around the grounds. They left around noon to head to the winery. When they arrived, Dean put his arm out to escort Alex inside. All eyes were on them as they walked into the tasting.

"Everyone is staring. Do I look that bad?"

"Quite the contrary, baby. You are the most stunningly beautiful woman in the room. And I am lucky enough to have you on my arm."

Alex smiled as they were taken to their table. A waiter came with a tray of small plastic cups, filled with different types of wine, as well as a cheese and cracker spread. Dean and Alex sampled all the different wines and finished their food.

"So, Alex, which one was your favorite?"

"I've always been partial to white wine. Moscato has alway been my favorite."

"I think that we should buy a couple bottles on our way out. I would love to have a glass of wine in front of the fireplace with you."

"I bet we could think of some other things to do in front of the fireplace."

"In due time my love, but first, I thought may you'd be up for a drive around the town?"

"I'd love to. I just love spending time with you, even when we're not naked."

Dean lovingly caressed her face.

"When we stop to buy the wine, could we see if they have any of those cheese and cracker plates for sale, in case we get hungry?"

"And how might we work up an appetite, my love?"

"You'll see, Dean."

Dean laughed as they headed out to the shop. Dean grabbed two bottles of Moscato and a snack tray, paid then they headed out to his truck. They spent a couple of hours taking a scenic driving tour of Lakeside, the town their resort was located in. Dean stopped at an overlook and parked. They got out and sat on one of the benches. Dean put an arm around Alex as she laid her head on his shoulder.

"This view is breathtaking. Thank you for bringing me here. I love you," she whispered.

"Not as breathtaking as you. Alexandra, I love you."

Dean kissed her tenderly, making her heart start racing.

"I am truly in this for the long haul, Dean. I can't stand the thought of not being with you. Please, baby, don't break my heart again."

"Alexandra, my love, I promise you that I will love you for the rest of our days on this earth. Let's head back to the cabin so I can show you how much I love you. I need to make love to you, baby."

"Mmm, let's go. I want you."

They got back in the Dean's truck and headed back to the cabin. As soon as they were inside, they started tearing each others' clothes off, leaving a trail from the door to the rug in front of the fireplace. They laid down and Dean took Alex into his arms. He kissed her mouth hard as he slipped a couple of fingers inside her pussy. She moaned into his mouth as her tongue tangled with his.

Dean started sucking hard on her neck. The sting felt incredible, and she felt her pussy get wet.

"Oh, baby, you must like that. I can feel how wet you are, baby."

Dean continued his tour of her body. He spent a gloriously long amount of time sucking on her breasts, leaving her nipples hard as diamonds.

"I can't get over how beautiful you are."

"Mmm, Dean."

Alex felt his tongue slide down her belly. He removed his fingers from her pussy and let his tongue take over. He slid his tongue up and down her pussy, lightly and slowly.

"Oh, Dean. You're driving me wild. Please, go harder."

Dean ignored her request, continuing his soft, slow teasing as she writhed beneath him.

"You're being naughty," she said as she gave him a light smack on his sexy ass.

"My, my, Alex, getting feisty, aren't you?."

Alex spanked him again, a little harder this time. Dean still continued to lick her slowly, building up the pressure in her pussy.

"Baby, I really want to be inside you now."

"I wanna try a new position. Tell me what to do."

"Mmm, this is going to be fun. Baby, go to the couch and kneel on it, using the back of it for support."

Alex did as she was told, excited for what would be coming next.

"Now spread you legs for me, baby."

Dean walked over to her and stood behind her, putting his hands on her hips. He slid his dick inside her pussy from behind. He started thrusting slowly and sensually.

"Oh, Dean, you feel so much deeper inside me this way, Oh fuck, this feels amazing. Dean, will you…" she let her voice trail off, suddenly feeling shy.

"Will I what, baby?"

"I'm afraid to ask."

"Baby, don't ever be afraid to tell me when you want something. I love a woman who knows what she wants."

"Spank me while you fuck my pussy."

"Oh, fuck, baby, that's so hot."

Dean lightly smacked her sexy bottom as he kept thrusting his dick into her. She felt his hand spank her again and a deep moan escaped her lips.

"I love the way your hand feels on my naked ass. I like getting spanked, baby. I feel like I'm going to orgasm soon, but I want this to last. Can you go even slower?"

Dean slowed his pace, making this last for almost an hour. Dean could feel her breathing become more rapid and knew she was close to exploding.

"Oh, Dean, I'm so close. Please fuck me harder, baby. Oh god, oh fuck, oh Dean. So fucking good, baby."

She screamed as another powerful orgasm left her entire body quaking. The power of her orgasm sent him flying and he exploded inside her, filling her pussy with his love juice.

"Alex, I think we need another shower after that."

"Yes, we do baby. I'm also starting to get a little tired, how about you?"

"Yeah, thanks to you, my dirty woman. Let's go shower then head to bed. We have a lot more fun in store for tomorrow."

Chapter Thirteen

Dean and Alex woke up the following morning, completely famished from the previous day's activities. They headed out to grab some breakfast.

"What would you like to do today, my angel?"

Alex felt a naughty thought or two creep into her head, thinking about the basket that was back at the cabin, but she kept those to herself for now.

"When we were driving last night, I saw a place where you can go horseback riding. Would you be willing to do that?"

"I'm a bit surprised. I thought sure you would want to go back to the cabin and get naked. Horseback riding sounds like fun, then maybe some lunch afterwards."

"Oh, don't worry, I had some naughty thoughts too. That'll be for later," she said as she licked her lips slowly, causing him to nearly fall out of his chair.

After finishing breakfast, they headed to the farm where the horses were kept.

"I have to confess, I've never been horseback riding and I'm a little nervous."

"I promise, you'll be just fine. I've been riding all my life, so I'll guide you. The key thing is not to let your horse know you're scared. If you really don't feel comfortable, though, we can do something else."

"No, I want to try this. I know how much you love riding and I wanna be able to join you when we get back home."

Alex smiled as they headed inside to pick their horses. The owner lead them to the stables and got their horses ready. Alex climbed up on her horse, as Dean looked on in amazement at how easy she made that look. Not quite as easy for him, but he made it up with only a little bit of awkwardness. They headed out as Alex told him how to handle the reins. After about ten minutes, he felt more comfortable and really started to enjoy himself.

"You look so beautiful up there on that horse."

"Thanks. You look pretty damn handsome yourself."

After riding for about an hour, they reached a field of wildflowers.

"Wow, this is so beautiful. I could sit here all day and just gaze at the flowers."

"That's how I feel when I look at you. I love looking at you, especially when we're making love. You are by far the most stunning woman ever to walk this planet."

He leaned over and kissed her then pulled his phone out.

"Alex, we haven't taken any pictures together since I've moved back, and I think this is the perfect place for our first one."

He made sure to get both of the horses in the picture as well as the flowers.

"Wow, I don't usually care for pictures of myself, but I really like how this turned out. Thank you for capturing this moment. Are you ready to head back?"

"Yeah, baby, I really want to get you back to the cabin. I need your naked body in my arms, baby."

Alex smiled, as they headed back to the stable. Once they returned the horses, they started the drive back to the cabin.

"Do you want to stop and get some lunch on the way?"

"No. What I'm hungry for right now is you. I really want to get back and see what else is in that basket," she said eagerly.

Dean quickly raced back to the cabin. They went inside and headed straight to the bedroom. He brought the basket over to the bed so they look together.

"I know what I want."

"Do tell, baby."

"I want you to tie my wrists to the bed and blindfold me. The thought of that excites me."

"You did it again."

"What?"

"Your naughty words and your sexy sultry voice was all it took to get my dick hard. Look at my jeans, babe."

Alex looked down and noticed Dean would rip a hole in his crotch if those jeans didn't come off now. Much to his delight, she unbuttoned and unzipped his pants and slid them down, along with his underwear. After he stepped out of them, he removed the rest of his clothing while Alex followed suit.

She watched Dean take the scarves and blindfold out of the basket and return it to the table.

"Baby, slide up to the head of the bed, so I can tie your wrists to the headboard."

Alex did as he requested, feeling her pussy dripping as Dean bound her to the bed. He put the blindfold in place so Alex could no longer see where he was or what he was doing.

After several minutes, Alex felt Dean's hands on her legs as he gently spread them. One leg at a time, he ran his tongue up and down from hip to ankle as she writhed on the bed. Alex wanted nothing more than to move his hands where she most wanted them, but she couldn't. The feeling of his tongue so close to her pussy was driving her wild.

"Fuck, I want you so bad, my sexy man."

She heard Dean groan deeply as he moved his hands under her ass, squeezing hard. She loved the feeling of his body heat, his naked skin so close to hers. She moaned softly, eagerly anticipating the moment he would touch her where she most wanted him to, but he made her wait. He slid his hands to waist, teasing her belly with his fingers. The feeling of his breath on her skin sent chills through her entire body.

She could feel him moving on the bed, but still couldn't see anything. Suddenly, his lips lightly brusher hers. He felt her mouth open, so he slid his tongue inside and interlaced it with hers. As quickly as he started kissing her, he stopped. She felt his lips on her neck, sucking hard. The sting of it was exciting her even more. He had always been so gentle with her, but this slightly rougher side was amazing. Dean move down to her breasts. He ran his tongue all over her beautiful D-cups, stopping to suck on her nipples. The sensation was almost too much to handle.

She cried out, "Please fuck me now."

"In due time, my love."

She felt him moving, again unsure where he was. He had moved on top of her, supporting his weight with his hands. She could feel his huge dick light brushing her pussy as he lowered his head and kissed her hard. She joined her tongue to his, returning his intense passion. He moved down her body until his head was near her pussy. Alex felt him gently blowing his warm breath on her pussy, a feeling like nothing she'd ever know.

Dean moved his head closer to her, and ran his tongue along her inner thighs. Again, she started writhing on the bed, trying to get his mouth on her pussy.

"Please, I don't know much more I can stand. I need you to touch me now, baby. I'm so wet, please, baby, please I need to feel you inside me."

"Soon, baby, I promise, but first, I want to taste you."

Dean lowered his head and covered her pussy with his mouth, flicking her clit lightly with his tongue.

"Oh fuck, that feels so good."

Dean didn't respond and instead kept licking her clit, increasing the intensity. He felt her struggling to free her hands.

"I really need to touch you."

"I know, but I'm in charge so you'll do what I tell you to do."

"Mmmm, so fuckin' hot."

Dean licked harder and harder until he felt his goddess explode in another earth-shattering orgasm, moaning loudly as her body quaked with ecstasy. While her pussy was at its most sensitive, he slid up her body and entered her with his rock hard cock.

"Mmmm, so good, Dean."

She felt him sliding his dick in and out slowly and passionately, as she ached to wrap her arms around him. As he moved closer to his own orgasm, his thrusts became more powerful until she heard him emit a low, guttural growl, filling her pussy with a huge load of his hot cream.

"Fuck, every time I'm inside you is more incredible. My dick has never been this satisfied. I love you."

"I love you so much. I don't know what I would do if I ever lost you again."

"Please don't worry, that won't happen Now, baby, tell me how that felt."

"Okay, but could you remove the blindfold and untie me first. I want to be able to look at you and touch you."

Dean did as she asked then laid down next to her. Alex laid in his arms, her head on his chest.

"Dean, that was unlike anything I've ever experienced. Not being able to see you or touch you was exciting. I loved not knowing where you were or what you would be doing next. It seemed like all my other senses were enhanced, especially between my legs. Thank you for being someone that I can trust with my naughtiest desires. But now, it's my turn to pleasure you."

"What do you have in mind, my sexy tigress?"

"Are you willing to be tied and blindfolded like I was?"

"Oh fuck yeah, baby. I've never had a woman do that to me before. I love that you will be the first."

Alex flashed a naughty smile as she bound his wrists to the bed and slipped the blindfold over his eyes. She walked over to the basket and found a soft feather. This will be fun to tease him with, she thought to herself. She didn't move for several minutes, just watching her man lying there completely naked. She watched in awe as his erection grew larger. She walked over to the bed and lightly tickled his balls with the feather.

"Oh, baby," she heard him moan.

Alex took the feather and started sliding it up and down his dick, as his moaning intensified. She started teasing his chest next.

"Baby, that feels so good. I really want to feel your fingers on me."

"When I say it's time. Remember, I'm in charge now."

Alex climbed onto the bed and straddled her sexy cowboy. He felt her breasts brushing his chest, the feeling of her hard nipples sending shivers through his body. He felt her lips on his chest, showering him with kisses, then using her tongue to tease his nipples. Fuck, this woman drove him wild. She slid down his body, making sure her breasts kept touching him until she was at his dick. Instead of stopping there, she moved down to his legs and started sucking the insides of his thighs.

What are you doing to me, baby? My cock is aching for you, you naughty little tease."

Alex loved the effect she was having on him. She took her fingers and started lightly tickling his balls as he growled. She knew what he wanted most by the way he kept moving his ass. She knew she had tortured him enough, so she slid her body back up and took his dick into her mouth. She slid her lips and tongue along his shaft with just enough pressure to get him groaning again. After a few minutes, she stopped.

"Baby, please don't stop."

Alex didn't respond and instead took his balls in her mouth, lightly sucking and licking them. No woman had ever been willing to do that before and he couldn't believe how incredible it felt.

"OH FUCK, BABY! SO FUCKING GOOD."

Alex moved back to his dick, sucking harder and faster until Dean filled her mouth with hot cum, which she happily swallowed. Alex licked the head of Dean's hot dick, cleaning the rest of his man-juice off. Feeling her mouth got him hard again.

"Well, well, looks like my work here isn't finished."

She mounted her lover, taking his dick deep inside her. Since Dean's hands were still tied up, she used his torso to brace herself. Alex bounced up and down on Dean's cock slowly, taking him in as deep as she could. She moaned loudly, matching his animal-like growls.

"You feel so fucking good inside me. I love you so much."

"Oh, baby, you're incredible. I'm picturing those sexy breasts bouncing while you fuck me. Please baby, go harder. I want to fill that hot pussy with my cum."

Alex rode harder and harder until they both exploded. She reached up and untied Dean's hands and he removed the blindfold. Alex collapsed down on his chest, completely spent. Dean held her tight, both of them breathing heavily, their sweat-soaked bodies pressed against other in pure ecstasy.

"Baby, this has been an absolutely incredible day, but I am completely famished. How about we take a hot steamy shower together than go out and have dinner?"

"I'm starving, so that sounds great. It's tough work riding my sexy cowboy," she said with a wink and a naughty smile.

After a long, luxurious shower, they headed out for dinner. Dean took them to an Italian restaurant he saw when they were driving around. After enjoying dinner and a glass of wine, they drove back to the cabin.

Dean asked, "How would you like to take a moonlit boat ride then a stroll around the resort?"

"I would love to."

They walked down to the lake where a rowboat was waiting for them. He helped Alex in then climbed in himself and rowed to the middle of the lake. They leaned in and kissed passionately as the full moon shone down on them. They sat and enjoyed the view for a while then Dean rowed them back to the dock. He got out then held the boat steady for Alex. After he secured the boat, they headed out to the walking path, holding hands like a couple of teenagers. As they were walking, they found a small lake with benches around it. Dean walked Alex over to one of the benches and sat down. He pulled Alex into his arms and kissed her. They spent the next hour sitting on the bench, kissing, completely lost in each other. They walked the rest of the way around the lake before heading back to the cabin. All that kissing had Alex worked up.

"Can we please go back to bed and fuck some more?"

"Now why would I want to do that?" he said with a wink.

They headed upstairs, eagerly undressed each other and spent the rest of the night naked, in each others' arms making love until they were so exhausted they fell asleep still holding each other.

Chapter Fourteen

Alex was awakened in the morning by a tender kiss on her lips. "Mmmm, that's so much better than being woken up by an alarm. I love feeling your sexy lips on mine."

"I hated to wake you, but I have something special planned for our last day in the Poconos. I saw a brochure for hot air balloon rides, and thought that would be romantic. I thought we could do that and then maybe a special picnic in one of the beautiful parks near the balloon launch."

"Wow, I've never been in a balloon before. I must admit I'm a little scared, but I want to try it."

"I've always wanted to try it myself. I am so thankful I never did any of this stuff. I love that we are getting to share so many new things with each other."

"I feel the same way. I've loved everything we've done together so far. I hope we have a lot more adventures together."

"I promise you, baby, we will. Now, let's go get showered, grab a quick breakfast and head out for our next adventure."

After showering together, they got dressed and stopped by a small cafe for breakfast before heading to the balloon launch. Alex was excited but also trying to keep her nerves in check. She wasn't particularly afraid of heights but this was something she'd never done before. She knew, though, that Dean would be right there with her, holding her, so she knew she would be fine. They arrived and headed inside to pay. Dean booked them a private ride, so they wouldn't have anyone else with them except for their operator, David.

David walked them out to the launch area. Alex smiled when she saw Dean had picked a balloon with two intertwined hearts on it.

"I picked this one to celebrate our love, my angel."

"I love you so much. Thank you."

"I can definitely tell you two are meant to be," David told them with a smile. "Are you ready to begin your adventure?"

Dean and Alex both responded with a yes, so David opened the door and they all entered the balloon, David closing and latching the door behind them. After running through a few rules and instructions with them, he prepared for takeoff. As they rose higher and higher into the sky, Alex couldn't help but notice how breathtaking the view was, a huge smile sweeping across her face. Dean put an arm around her waist.

"Are you doing okay?"

Resting her head on his strong shoulder, Alex replied, "Yes. I was nervous about nothing. This is absolutely incredible."

They spent the rest of the ride like that, enjoying not only the beautiful aerial tour, but enjoying being with the person they were put on this planet to love. The tour lasted about 90 minutes, though it felt like it was much shorter. Alex was so thankful she didn't chicken out, as this was truly a magical experience. When they landed, David opened the door and they exited the balloon. Dean thanked him and handed him a tip then took Alex's hand as they walked back to his truck.

"Now on to our next destination, my love."

"When on earth did you have time to plan all this?"

"I booked everything once you agreed to go away with me. I really wanted to make our first trip together a memorable one."

"You definitely exceeded that goal, my love. I feel like a queen when I'm with you."

"As you should, Queen Alexandra," Dean said as he bowed before her.

Alex smiled and gave him a playful punch on the arm. Dean stopped the truck in front of the same cafe where they had breakfast.

"I'll be right back, babe."

He disappeared inside the cafe and returned a few minutes later with a picnic basket and a bottle of wine, which he put on the back floor of the truck. He drove them to a beautiful park complete with a walking path and beautiful fountain. Dean parked and they walked to one of the picnic tables near the fountain. After they sat, Dean unpacked the basket.

"I grabbed us each a chicken Caesar salad, along with some homemade garlic bread."

Dean poured them each a glass of wine. He lifted his glass and Alex followed suit.

"A toast to the woman who I now know is my soul-mate. I love you, Queen Alexandra."

They clinked glasses and each took a sip.

"I love you, King Dean."

Dean smiled as they both began eating, never breaking eye contact. After they ate and finished off the entire bottle of wine, Dean took the basket back to the truck.

When he returned, he asked, "How about a romantic walk? The path covers the entire perimeter of the park."

Alex smiled and nodded her approval. Dean, always the gentleman, put out a hand and helped her up. Keeping her hand in his, they began their walk. The path was full of flowers in every color and variety you could think of and the view was spectacular.

When they reached the midpoint of the path, Dean stopped.

"How about a little rest before we keep going?"

Alex nodded and they both sat down in the grass. Dean moved a little so he was sitting behind Alex, his arms around her waist. She felt him start nuzzling her neck, and that familiar heat made another appearance between her thighs. She took each of his hands in hers, loving the feeling of his strong arms around her. Alex knew she wouldn't be able to go on living if she ever lost him, and that frightened her. She quickly perished that thought, as she didn't want anything to put a damper on this trip.

Dean laid back, gazing up at the sky. Alex joined him, her head resting on his chest. She sighed in contentment, lying here in her lover's arms. She lifted her head and kissed Dean passionately. Their tongues became interlaced, intensely dancing in their mouths, Kissing Dean always got her worked up and she couldn't help but think of that beautiful bed waiting for them back at the cabin.

"Shall we finish our walk?"

"In a moment, but first, what was that kiss for?"

"Because I love you and I'm having such a wonderful day."

Dean reached up and caressed her cheek lightly with his hand.

"I love you, Alex."

Dean got up and helped Alex up then they finished their walk around the path, stopping at the fountain when they were done. Dean took out his phone so he could grab a picture of them in front of the fountain.

"Okay, time for our next adventure."

"You are spoiling me way more than I deserve. Where are we headed next?"

"First and foremost, you absolutely deserve this. You are an amazing woman who deserves all the love in the world. Our next stop is another fun surprise I booked for us. You'll have to wait until we get there."

Alex smiled and started bouncing in the truck seat.

"What are you doing, baby?"

"I'm so excited about our next stop, I can't contain myself," she said laughing as she bounced even harder.

Dean laughed out loud, loving this lighthearted side of her. Alex was so serious when he first returned. He knew it was because of how much he'd hurt her but now that they had rediscovered their love for on another, she was smiling and laughing more often than not. Dean would never tire of the sound of her laughter. A little while later, he pulled the truck to a stop at a small train depot.

"I rented us a trolley to tour the mountain area of Lakeside."

"Oh, that sounds so romantic."

They walked inside the depot and were led to their trolley. Just as Dean had requested, there was a bottle of wine, a cheese plate, and a beautiful bouquet of yellow daisies on the dining table. Dean looked at Alex and saw her eyes filling with tears.

"Is everything okay, baby? Why are you crying?"

"I'm just so happy, I can't hold back the tears. Every time I think you're done surprising me, you get me again."

"Baby, it makes me so happy to hear you say that. Now, how about we take a seat and enjoy our tour?"

"That sounds perfect."

The conductor started the trolley then put some romantic music on before starting the ride. Dean and Alex sat side by side, holding each other. They wanted to dance, but had to remain seated for the ride, so they swayed together in their seat. The scenery was beautiful, but mostly what Alex and Dean saw was each others' eyes.

When the ride was over, she whispered, "I bet this was beautiful, but I have to confess all I saw was your handsome face."

Dean kissed the top of her head and replied, "Don't worry, baby, all I saw was your beautiful face, so we're even."

Alex smiled warmly and Dean's heart almost burst with the love he felt for her. When the trolley came to a stop, they disembarked and headed to Dean's truck.

"One last stop before we head back to the cabin for our last night here. I have a very special dinner planned for you. Don't ask me any questions, as I'll refuse to answer."

"Ooh, I'm so excited. Let's go!"

Dean made a stop at a restaurant and came back out with a large bag. Alex was dying to ask him a ton of questions but she knew it would be fruitless, so she just sat there with a big, bright smile on her face. After about a half-hour, Dean pulled up and parked in front of a fenced in area. He parked and grabbed the bag then came around and opened Alex's door for her. Hand-in-hand, they walked up to the gate and went inside. There was a beautiful glass table and two cast-iron chairs. Alex also saw a beautiful, king-sized canopy bed. "There's a bed. I mean, I know you can see there's a bed, but..."

"Alex, this is completely private and absolutely allowed. We will be making love in that bed tonight, under the moon and the stars. But first, let's enjoy some dinner."

Dean pulled out Alex's chair and pushed it in once she sat down. He joined her and served them each dinner and a glass of wine. He lit the tapers in the center of the table and put some romantic music on his phone.

"The candlelight makes you look even more beautiful."

"You're so sweet. I love you."

"I love you, my angel."

After they ate, Dean walked over to Alex and put his hand out. When she stood, Dean wrapped her in his arms and they started dancing slowly, loving the feeling of their bodies pressed against each other. As they swayed together, Dean felt himself starting to get hard. Damn, this woman must have a remote control for my cock he thought to himself.

"Oh, my, I guess you're enjoying our dance."

"I am but now I think it's time we engage in our favorite dance. Baby, I want to make love to you right here, right now, under this beautiful sky."

Alex didn't respond and instead took his hand and led him to the bed. Alex slid her hands under Dean's shirt, tickling his chest with her fingers as she lifted his shirt off. She opened his pants and removed them along with his underwear. She would never tire of his chiseled, muscular body. Dean bent down and removed his boots and socks.

"Dean, please lay on the bed and wait for me."

She walked to the table, grabbed his phone and put on one of her favorite naughty rock songs then returned to the bed. She bent down and removed her shoes and socks. She slowly and sensually lifted her shirt off. One notch at a time, she slowly opened and removed her bra, running her hands over her breasts as she licked her lips.

"Holy shit, baby, you're so fuckin' sexy."

Alex flashed him the sexiest sideways glance he'd ever seen as she removed her pants and panties. Now completely naked like her lover, she joined him on the bed.

"Do you have any idea how fucking sexy that was?"

She smiled then leaned over and kissed him, jamming her tongue eagerly into his mouth. He interlaced his tongue with hers, kissing her passionately as he felt her naked skin against his own.

Alex pushed him on his back, climbed on top of him and lowered her body onto his, taking his hard cock deep inside her. She sat up straight, giving Dean the full view of her incredible curves as she slowly rode her sexy cowboy.

"Oh Dean, you feel so good, baby."

Dean wrapped his arms around her and rolled her onto her back, his dick never leaving her pussy.

Dean slid his dick in and out of her with the same slow passion that she used on him. They slowly and sensually made love for hours. Being outside made their lovemaking even more primal. The cool, spring night was quiet, except for the sounds of two lovers moaning with pleasure, completely consumed by the pure ecstasy of their passion. Their hearts, minds, souls, and bodies had truly become one as they reached that magical apex together, moaning loudly as they rode wave after wave of intense rapture.

"My queen, would you like to sleep here tonight?"

"Oh my, yes, my king, it would be my pleasure."

Completely spent from their action-packed day and night of incredible lovemaking, Dean pulled the covers up and pulled Alex close, kissing her goodnight as they drifted off to sleep, still naked, holding each other tight.

Chapter Fifteen

Alex and Dean were awakened the following morning by the beautiful sound of birds singing. Unfortunately, it was time to head back to reality. They returned to the cabin to pack their stuff, including the contents of their goodie basket, and head back to Lancaster. Dean promised Alex they would definitely get plenty of use out of their naughty new toys. After stopping for breakfast, they got back on the road. When they got back home, they ran over to Hannah's to pick up Holly then Dean drove Alex to her farm so she could unpack and grab a shower.

"Headin' over to the market today?"

"No need. I arranged to have a couple of my workers cover today."

"Cool, then you're mine today."

"Mmmm."

"I'll be back after I unpack and shower. Wanna grab some lunch?"

"I'd rather grab your dick."

"Naughty girl."

She smiled wickedly at her sexy man, imagining all the dirty things she wanted to do to him today. She fully intended to make use of some of the toys that were in their basket not to mention she might have a sexy surprise or two brewing in that dirty mind of hers. His voice snapped her back to the present.

"I'll be back in about an hour, babe."

"Can't wait. Oh, don't forget to bring the basket."

"Damn woman!"

She started rubbing his ass, so damn sexy in those tight jeans he was wearing. He let a low growl escape his lips as he pulled in close for a kiss. She loved feeling his sexy, pouty lips against hers, his tongue exploring her mouth, though she preferred when that tongue was exploring somewhere else.

"Hurry back. I'm really hungry."

"I noticed!"

Dean waved as he got in his truck and headed home. He quickly unpacked and showered, then grabbed what he needed to spend the night at Alex's house. He had a feeling it was going to be a hot, hot night. Alex was waiting on her porch when he pulled up. She was in tight jeans and a low-cut white t-shirt that looked incredible against her sun-kissed skin. And holy shit, the cleavage she was showing was threatening to rip his zipper. Fuck, that woman was hotter than hell.

Somehow, they both made it through lunch without tearing their clothes off. The same could not be said when they got back to Alex's house. There was a trail of clothes leading to her bedroom. Dean pulled her into a tight embrace. She could feel his erection against her and it had her dripping wet. She wanted him so damn bad and she was feeling especially naughty today.

"Get on the bed and close your eyes."

Dean laid down, anxiously awaiting her touch. She walked over to her dresser and took a spoonful of icing out a bowl she had hidden before he got back. She spread the icing on his sexy chest, then straddled him and started licking the icing off his chest. The feeling of her tongue on his skin was driving him wild. He loved watching those sexy breasts bouncing as she kept licking him. He gave her a playful swat on her sexy ass, causing her to moan in pleasure.

"Did you like that?"

"Yeah, baby. It's sexy."

Once she had licked every last bit of icing off, she worked her way down, tracing his happy trail with her tongue, getting closer and closer to where he most wanted to feel that sexy mouth. Much to his delight, she moved down a little lower and took every inch of his erection into her mouth. She slid her lips and tongue up and down slowly. The pleasure she was able to give him was unlike any woman he'd ever known. She stopped and laid down next to him, spreading her legs wide.

"Tell me what you want."

"Please come put that hot tongue in my pussy."

Dean moved on top of her and licked a trail down her body, starting between her breasts until he reached her abdomen. She was writhing, desperately trying to get his tongue where she most wanted it. Time to tease her a bit, he thought to himself.

"If you don't stop that, you won't get to feel my tongue."

She stopped moving immediately as she licked her lips. He could tell how bad she wanted him. Instead of giving her what she wanted, he started kissing and sucking the insides of her thighs. She started writhing again.

"Remember what I just told you."

She stopped again. He kept licking, kissing and sucking her everywhere but that hot pussy. He could tell she was fighting hard not to move. She was moaning like crazy and breathing hard. He finally decided he'd tortured her enough and put his head between her sexy legs. She moaned loudly when his tongue made contact with her pussy, setting her entire body on fire.

"Oh, that feels so fuckin' good."

He smiled when he noticed she was still trying not to move.

"Baby, you may move now."

"Oh, thank god, I wasn't sure how much longer I could last."

He didn't answer as he was busy using his mouth for something much more fun. He loved how she tasted, loved the flowery fragrance of her shower gel, the softness of her skin. There truly was nobody like his goddess. He saw her arch her back as her body began to quake. He knew he had her close, so he started sucking on her clit until she screamed, her entire body shaking like an earthquake.

"Fuck, that was amazing. Please, baby, get up here and fuck my pussy."

He growled as he slid up her sexy body and slid his dick deep inside her, slowly sliding in and out. He put his hands under her sexy ass and lifted her hips so he could get even deeper inside her. She ran her finger-nails up and down his back as he continued his powerful thrusts. She was still sensitive from the orgasm he brought her so the feeling of his dick rubbing against her clit was magnified and she felt her body start quivering again.

"Oh, Dean, holy shit, oh fuck, baby, so good."

Hearing her dirty talk, feeling her body explode sent him over the edge and he filled her with a huge load of his warm cream.

"So good, my goddess."

Dean moved next to her as they both laid close together, breathing hard after that incredible sex. He was far from done with her though, and lucky for him, she was still horny as hell. After a few minutes, she looked into his eyes. What she said next quickly awakened the snake and he was rock hard again.

"I wanna ride you. NOW!"

Before he even had a chance to respond, she was on top of him, sliding up and down his cock. She lowered her mouth onto his and kissed him harder than any woman before her. She jammed her tongue into his mouth with such passion that he almost shot his load. He took a couple deep breaths as his tongue found hers. After a couple minutes she sat up, leaning back to get just the angle she needed. She could feel his huge cock stroking her g-spot. Her body was so hot, she felt like she was sitting on the sun.

She rode him hard and fast, the friction making her pussy feel like never before. He matched her with his powerful thrusts until she took off for outer space, as she showered his dick with her sweet juice. She loved when her orgasms were so intense that she squirted and it felt more incredible than anything she'd ever felt. She slowed down as the pleasure was almost too intense. Dean let out a deep, guttural growl from deep down as he filled her with another huge load. She barely had the energy left to climb off him but managed to lay down next to him.

Dean pulled her in close and she put her head on his sexy chest. He put his hand under her chin, gently lifted her head and kissed her lovingly.

"I love you, Alex."

"I love you too, Dean."

Feeling completely exhausted, he pulled the covers up. They quickly fell asleep holding each other. After a nice long nap, they both started to stir, stomachs growling from their oh-so-pleasurable workout. Dean kissed the top of Alex's head and she sighed contentedly.

"Hungry, babe?"

"Starving."

"Any idea what you want to eat?"

"Oh, maybe some eggplant," she said with a naughty wink.

"Oh it's like that, huh?"

"Yeah!"

"Then I want to suck that juicy peach."

"Mmmm, yes please."

"Seriously though, my stomach is growling."

"Like you were earlier?"

"Hey, you weren't exactly quiet, babe!"

"Your fault with that hot tongue and sexy dick."

"Fuck, babe, you drive me crazy!"

"I try!"

"Now, dinner, please."

"I could go for some Italian."

"Sounds good."

After showering, together of course, they got dressed and headed to the one Italian restaurant in the area. They ordered their meals and wine, then sat and talked while they waited for the food to arrive.

"I had so much fun on our getaway. Thanks for taking me."

"My pleasure, babe."

"Mmm, mine too!"

"Whatcha wanna do after dinner?"

Dean saw a naughty smile appear on her face.

"I think we need to get the basket out."

"Yeah, plus I need to do somethin'."

"What?"

"You'll see or maybe you won't."

She was about to ask what he meant by that when their waiter appeared with their wine. He poured them each a glass and let them know their meals would be out shortly.

"What did you mean by that."

"No more questions."

"Meanie!"

"Keep that up, and it's TV for the rest of the night."

Alex made the motion of zipping her lips, as she laughed. He never got tired of hearing that sound. He loved her laugh, especially when she was laughing in delight during sex. He started imagining what it would be like to be married, something he always wanted to do. He knew for sure she was the one he wanted to spend the rest of his life with. Might have to do some ring shopping, he thought to himself.

Alex was watching him, wondering what put that dreamy look on his face. He was probably thinking about what he plans to do to me in bed tonight. She loved this man so much and she knew for sure she never wanted to be without him again. She shuddered for a second, thinking how close she was to losing him after what Tyler did but quickly put that out of her head.

A couple minutes later, their dinner arrived. After they finished eating, they shared a sinful dessert, and of course, all she could think about was eating it off his sexy chest. That was all it took and she started getting wet. She couldn't wait until they got back home! Once their waiter brought the check and bagged up the rest of their bottle of wine, they paid and headed out.

"How about we pick up Holly and take her to the park for a bit?"

"Okay, I guess."

"You guess? Did you have something else in mind?"

"Yep! Still craving some eggplant."

Dean smiled. He knew how lucky he was to have a woman so into sex. Not all guys could say that and he knew for sure he would never screw things up with her again. They headed back to Alex's, picked up Holly and drove to the dog park. When they got there, they were happy to see Chris and his family there. They walked in and let Holly off her leash. She ran over to where Daisy and Chris's girls were playing and started chasing each other while the girls laughed and threw tennis balls for them.

Alex and Dean sat down on the bench next to Chris and Tracey. Chris loved seeing the two of them together and looking so happy.

"So, I have some updates on Tyler."

Dean responded, "Do we wanna know?"

"In this case, yeah. Rest assure you'll never have to worry about him again. He's been tied to even more cases similar to what he did to you. Plus, they've been able to link him to a few unsolved murders as well. I don't expect him to ever see the light of day again."

Alex's eyes filled with tears, which quickly spilled over.

"What's wrong, baby?"

"It just scared me hearing how he had possibly killed. I don't know what I would have done if he escalated things with you."

"But he didn't. It scares me hearing it too, but we just need to focus on what did happen. I'm here and I'm more in love with you now than I've ever been."

Alex smiled through the tears, as she quickly wiped them away. She looked over at Chris, grateful for everything he'd done for them. A few minutes later, one of his daughters ran over to let Alex know she needed to go cleanup after Holly. Turns out the girls were willing to do any part of taking care of a dog except that, Chris told them, laughing. They all joined in his laughter as Alex walked over to take care of things.

They spent another hour in the park before both dogs laid down, completely spent from playing and running. Alex and Tracey carried their leashes over and secured the dogs while the girls collected the tennis balls they had brought. While they had a few minutes alone, Dean told Chris he was starting to think about proposing to Alex and asked him if he would go with him to help pick out the ring. He also told Chris he wanted him to be his best man if they did get married.

"I would be honored, my friend."

Tracey and Alex were heading back, so they quickly changed the subject as he wanted to surprise Alex when he was ready to actually ask her. The girls asked if they could hold the leashes so Tracey told them to make sure they held on tight. They all walked out together, the girls a few steps ahead with the dogs. Dean opened his truck door so Holly could jump in, as Chris did the same for Daisy. They all hugged goodbye and headed home.

Alex was getting anxious to get home and see what Dean had in store for her. They went in and practically knocked each other over trying to get to the bedroom. Dean walked over to her with a dead serious look on his face.

"You were giving the orders earlier. Now it's my turn."

"Mmmm."

"Strip and get that sexy little ass on the bed."

Never breaking eye contact, she quickly stripped and laid down.

"Close those sexy eyes."

Alex closed her eyes, eagerly waiting for what was next. She was wetter than Niagara Falls at this point. She heard some rustling around but had no idea what Dean was up to. A few minutes later, she felt him get on the bed. She started to reach out her hand to touch him but he stopped her.

"Only when I tell you to."

"Okay."

She felt something being spread on her breasts and suddenly got a whiff of chocolate. He found where she hid the bowl of icing, she thought to herself. She couldn't wait to feel his tongue on her, licking it off. She felt his mouth on her left breast, sucking as his tongue teased her nipple until all the icing was gone. He repeated the same on her right breast, as she felt like she was going to explode. She felt him get off the bed.

"Keep those eyes closed, babe."

He returned a couple minutes later and laid down next to her. She heard a buzzing sound and knew what was coming. She felt the vibrator touch her clit and she almost hit the ceiling, the pleasure was so intense.

"Oh, god, that's amazing."

He turned the speed all the way up and kept it pressed to her clit until she was quivering from head to toe, screaming so loud, you could probably hear her all the way in New Jersey. He wouldn't remove the vibrator from her clit, making her explode again and again, until she couldn't stand it.

"Holy shit, Dean."

He still wouldn't remove the vibrator from her clit, as her body bucked and writhed with an intensity like nothing he'd ever seen until she drenched his hand.

"HOLY. FUCKIN' HELL."

"You can open your eyes now."

"I can't even begin to describe how that felt."

"Baby, that was so fuckin' hot. My dick is so fuckin' hard, that I need to fuck you now."

"Oh, god, please but could we try a new position?"

"Damn, woman. Lay on your side, babe."

Alex did as she was instructed. Dean climbed on the bed and laid behind her, lifting her leg so he could enter her. She felt his dick slide inside her pussy from behind and she gasped, it felt so damn good. His thrusts were strong and powerful, rocking her entire body, sending her into another universe. He pounded her harder and harder until she felt her pussy fill up with his cum as he groaned loudly.

"Oh Dean," were the only words her brain could remember.

"I'm completely spent, babe."

"Me too."

"Be right back."

Dean took Holly out to do her bedtime business then turned all the lights off and locked up before returning to bed. He was easily the sweetest man she'd ever known and she never stopped being grateful that they found their way back to each other. Dean joined her back in bed and pulled the covers up. He kissed her goodnight and they quickly fell asleep, completely spent and completely sated.

Chapter Sixteen

The rest of the week flew by and Friday morning had finally arrived. Alex loved what she did, loved working at the market, but she was always thankful that she could take weekends off. She and Dean were enjoying a much needed breakfast after another night of naked workouts in her bed.

"Babe, I have an idea for tonight."

"What?"

"How does dinner and a visit to the club sound?"

"I'd love to. I definitely love what happened the first time we there together."

"Me too. The stories that couch could tell."

"Mmmm, yeah."

"Hey, do you mind if I hang here while you hit the market?"

"Of course not."

"Cool."

She couldn't help but notice Dean looked like he was up to something, but she didn't ask. If was planning a surprise for her, she certainly wouldn't want to ruin it. She definitely loved the types of surprises he always had for her. After they were both showered and dressed, Dean helped her load her car and watched as she headed out. If she only knew what he was up to today. He would be meeting Chris and the rest of the

Dirty Girl Club at the local jeweler so he could pick out an engagement ring for his love. He hadn't yet decided on when or how he would be proposing but he wanted to have the ring ready. The girls knew her taste and ring size, so they could make sure that she would love what he picked out.

It only took about a half-hour and they found the one. The girls told Dean about her love of butterflies, so he picked out a butterfly setting with a one-carat diamonds in the middle, and came with a wedding band that interlocked with the engagement ring. He gave Chris the little velvet box to hide at his house so Alex would never accidentally stumble on it. Everyone promised not to let anything slip to Alex and they parted ways. Dean had a few more things to take care of. He was planning something special for Saturday night. Once he was done, he headed to his farm to get everything ready.

While Dean was out and about planning his surprises, Alex had arrived at the market, unloaded her car and got everything setup. When she had a lull in customers, she walked over to where Tyler's stand was. She was happy to see Hannah there starting to get things ready.

"Hey Hannah! So glad to see you here."

"Thanks for the tip, girl."

"Any time. If you ever need any help, let me know."

"I could use one small favor."

"Sure, what?"

"Could I put some flyers about my booth at yours so people know I'm here?"

"Absolutely. I get a pretty decent amount of traffic, so hopefully I can drive some of that your way."

"Thanks. I'll bring them by once I get them from the printer."

"Awesome. I better get back, seems like the lull is over."

Alex headed back to her booth and had a steady stream of customers for most of the day, never getting a chance to even stop for lunch. Mid-afternoon was here and she was starving. She was about to shut the booth when she saw Dean come walking down with a couple slices of pizza and a couple sodas.

"You're a lifesaver," Alex said as Dean handed her a slice and a drink.

"Had a feeling you'd be busy, so once I got done some stuff, I decided to come buy my babe some lunch."

Dean spent the rest of the time there with her, helping her finish up sales for the day then loading up her car to head home. He followed her to his house and they went inside to get ready to go out. Dean showered first then went down to sit on her porch while she got ready. He almost fell off his chair when she came down, his jaw hitting the ground. His goddess was dressed in tight jeans and a low-cut white t-shirt. The contrast of the shirt to her tan skin and red hair was breathtaking. He let out a loud whistle and her cheeks turn bright red, as a smile again appeared on her face.

"Something you like?"

"Holy shit, woman, so damn sexy. That shirt really shows off your, um, assets, babe."

"Naughty man," she said, laughing.

Dean wrapped his arms around her and kissed her passionately. They walked to his truck and headed to dinner then off to the club, where a couple of up-and-coming local bands were scheduled to perform. They came in and sat at Alex's reserved table. She was thankful that Uncle Jake allowed that to continue to be hers. Jake's son came over to say hello.

"Hey Alex."

"Hey Doug."

Looking at Dean, he said, "I hope you're okay, man. We all thought you were drunk until we got a request to view the security tapes. I'm sorry that happened."

"It's all good. He's in jail and I'm here with the woman of my dreams."

"Uncle Jake had told me about you two. He was sorry you split, so I can't wait to tell him you're back together."

"Thanks, man."

"Yeah, thanks, Doug," Alex added.

"I gotta run. Enjoy the show."

They sat through the first set, which was pretty great, full of harder, faster songs. When the second band came out, they were a little more subdued and when a ballad started, Dean asked Alex to dance. They walked out to the dance floor and Dean pulled her in close. She circled her arms around his chest and rested her head on his shoulder. They swayed together well past the end of the ballad, so lost in their love for one another, they never noticed the music speed up.

After a few songs, they sat down and each had a drink. Before they headed home, they asked Doug if they could check out the dressing room area. He walked them back and they headed to the room where they had first fucked. He held Alex close and kissed her hard, all the memories of that incredible night rushing back. The dance and their walk down memory lane had left them both feeling quite amorous, and so they beelined for her bedroom. Alex was about to remove her clothes when Dean stopped her.

"Allow me, my goddess."

Alex smiled as Dean lifted her shirt and removed it, his fingers softly teasing her skin, sending shivers up and down her spine. After removing her bra, he kissed her neck, and worked his way down to her breasts, teasing her nipples with his tongue. She felt him undo her jeans and slide them down along with her panties. She kicked her shoes off then stepped out of her jeans.

"My beautiful sun-kissed goddess."

He kissed her hard, his tongue in her mouth. She moaned into his mouth when she felt his fingers slip between her legs, lightly caressing her pussy. Damn, she was already wet. He felt her hands slide under his shirt and lift it off as she ran her soft hands all over his chest. She ran her fingers through his chest hair, driving him wild. She lightly raked her nails down his abs and opened his jeans, sliding them down, followed by his underwear. Her eyes immediately went to his erection and she licked her lips. He finished removing his clothes then pulled her into a tight embrace.

She ran her hands through his hair, down his back, and stopped on his ass, squeezing hard, causing him to growl like a tiger. Fuck, this woman was hot. He lowered his head and pressed his lips to hers. She opened for him and slid her tongue into his mouth, teasing his tongue with hers. He longed to feel that tongue on his dick and his balls. She was so fuckin' good at that.

As if she could read his mind, she said, "I really want to wrap my lips around your hot cock."

Dean walked over to the bed and laid down. Alex crawled up next to him, got on her hands and knees, and lowered her head, taking every inch of his dick in her mouth. She slid her soft sexy lips up and down his shaft. She took her tongue and swirled it around the tip like she was licking an ice cream cone. She replaced her mouth with her hand so she could gently suck on and lick his balls.

"Oh fuck, that feels so damn good, babe."

She ran her tongue along the vein between his balls, bringing him closer and closer to shooting his load. She could hear his breathing get heavier the more she teases his balls. She returned her mouth to his cock, sucking harder and faster until she felt him explode in her mouth. She loved how he tasted, as she swallowed every last drop, licking her lips as she kept eye contact with him. Her confidence in bed was one of the sexiest things about her.

"Mmmm, you're so delicious. I love drinking you, baby."

"My turn now. I need to taste that sweet pussy."

He heard the sexiest growl come out of her as she rolled onto her back, spreading her legs wide. She was so wet, and so ready to feel his tongue send her into orbit. Nobody knew how to pleasure her the way Dean did. He moved on top of her and kissed her passionately. His erection was resting on her pussy, getting her even wetter.

"Please, I need to feel you tongue between my legs. I'm so fuckin' hot for you."

He slowly dragged his tongue down her body as she quivered and writhed, dying to feel the pleasure awaiting her clit. He continued down her body until his head was between her legs. He licked her pussy hard, as he slid a couple fingers inside her, stroking her g-spot. He focused his tongue on her clit, as his fingers kept sliding in and out. She moaned loudly as her body started to take flight, moving closer and closer to orgasm. Dean increased the intensity of his tongue, stroking her g-spot even harder until he entire body took flight, gliding through the universe.

"Mmmm, oh Dean, oh so good. Oh shit, oh damn, oh fuck, so good. Don't stop. Please. Ahhhh...mmmm...I love you."

"Damn, babe, so sexy."

He laid on his back, dick so hard he could barely stand it. She moved on top of him, in reverse cowgirl. He held her hips to support as she bounced up and down, taking him deep inside her as he thrust his dick inside her. She leaned back and put her hands down to support herself.

"Please, baby, I wanna feel your hands on my breasts."

He gently started massaging her breasts, pinching her nipples. The sting combined with the intense pleasure of fucking him was incredible.

"Damn I love this view. Your ass is so damn sexy. I love watching your body bounce on mine."

"Your cock feels so damn incredible so deep inside me. Please, fill me with your luscious cream. I love that feeling of your cum shooting inside me. Oh, Dean, oh fuck."

She bounced harder and harder. The closer and close they moved to orgasm, the more the world around them disappeared. All that was left was each other. Naked, fucking, loving each other, screaming at their top of their lungs in ecstasy, both of them coming so hard the whole bed was shaking and banging into the wall. Once they came down off the cloud, Alex laid next to Dean, resting her head on his chest as he held her close. Being in his arms made her feel secure, feel loved, not to mention the naughty feelings.

They were both starving and completely wired after the incredible sex they just had, so they went out to the kitchen to grab a snack. They headed to the living room to watch some TV and quickly dozed off on the couch. They woke up an hour later and headed off to bed where they quickly fell into a deep sleep.

Chapter Seventeen

Alex woke up the next morning alone, her nose filling with a variety of delicious smells. She walked out to the kitchen and saw Dean standing there, sporting nothing but red silk boxers. Hot damn, she thought to herself. Not only is the sexiest man I've ever seen, he cooks too. She walked over and saw him cooking bacon, Holly sitting there just gazing at him. He also had eggs cooking and coffee brewing. He glanced over when he heard her enter the kitchen,

"Good morning, my beautiful goddess."

"Good morning. My kitchen smells delicious. Even more, it looks quite delicious."

"Down, woman. We at least need to eat first!"

Alex laughed as she walked over to the counter and poured two cups of coffee while Dean finished cooking. He put two plates together and brought them to the table. They sat down and enjoyed a delicious breakfast together while Holly sat there and drooled at the smell of the bacon.

"See, you're so sexy, all the women drool for you."

"Ha, ha, I think it's the bacon not me."

Alex pretended not to notice Dean slip Holly a piece of bacon. After they were done eating, Alex tried to do the dishes, but he wouldn't let her.

"You cooked me this amazing breakfast. The least I can do is cleanup."

"I have it covered."

She walked over and caressed his hot ass.

"Fine, but I will make it up to you later."

"You better!"

After they showered and dressed, they sat out on her porch while Holly wandered around, sniffing to see who'd visited overnight. Neither of them was taking until Dean caught her off-guard with a question.

"Will you help me pick out a horse?"

"That was out of the blue."

"I've been thinking about it since our trip. I had such a great time riding with you."

"Well, then I would love to. When did you want to go?"

"Now?"

"Okay. I know the perfect place. They will be able to fit you with the right saddle and the other equipment you'll need. And they are long-time friends of my dad, so they will give you a fair price."

"Awesome, babe."

"Are you okay with Holly riding in your truck? If not, I'll drive."

"Of course, I'm fine with it. Let's go!"

"Okay, we just need to hook my horse trailer up to your truck in case you find a horse you want."

"Okay."

He watched in awe as she hooked the trailer up without any help. He loved the tough side of her almost as much as that naughty side she brought to bed. She loved seeing how excited he was. Horseback riding was one of her favorite things to do, so she was happy he wanted to do it more often. They rode down to one of the farms that Alex dealt with due to their humane treatment of their animals. She showed him where to park and they headed to the tack shop, where the owner, George, was working.

"Miss Alex, great to see you."

She gave George a big hug and kiss on the cheek. He nodded toward Dean.

"And who might this be?"

"My boyfriend, Dean. He's interested in buying a horse. I taught him how to ride, and he fell in love with it."

George smiled, as horses were his passion.

"I'll take good care of him. Margie's in the kitchen if you and Holly wanna pop in."

Alex walked toward the house, knowing Dean would be in good hands. She knocked on the kitchen door and went in when she heard Margie yell to come in. Margie's face lit up when she saw them.

"Hello, sweetie. What brings you by?"

"Hi Margie. My boyfriend wants to buy a horse, so George is taking care of him."

"I'm so happy to hear you're seeing someone."

"This is the happiest I've been in a long time."

Margie, being the naughty woman she always was, asked, "Is he sexy?"

"Margie!"

"Guess I'll go see with my own eyes, then," she said with a wink.

Margie headed toward the barn, with Alex on her heels. She walked in and let out a low whistle. Turning to Alex, she smiled and said, "That's my girl, grabbed you a sexy one there."

Dean turned, a huge smile on his face, causing Margie to pretend to swoon.

"Lucky I love you, Alex, or I'd be tryin' to steal that fine man right out from under you."

Ever the charmer, Dean took her hand and kissed it. Every thing that man did made Alex love him even more. She and Margie returned to the house, saving Dean from any possible ass-pinching. They sat down at her kitchen table.

"Serious Margie here. I'm so happy to see you this happy, sweetie. We worried so much about you after your dad left this earth, and to see you this happy just makes my day. You're like the daughter I never had."

Tears filling her eyes, she replied, "I love you Margie."

Margie reached across the table and squeezed her hand. A few minutes later, George and Dean entered the kitchen.

"We're all set Miss Alex. We already put the equipment in the truck, so we just need to get Bryce into your trailer."

Margie and Alex turned their heads and looked at Dean, their eyes filling with tears. Without a word, Alex got up and wrapped her arms around Dean.

"Thank you. Bryce is a perfect name."

George went over and stood next to Margie, both of them smiling at how happy Alex was. They all walked outside to the trailer. Alex put Holly in the truck so she didn't startle the horse. George walked him out of the barn and handed the reins to Dean so he could lead him into the trailer. Once they had him secured, they hugged George and Margie goodbye and headed to Dean's house. Alex helped him get the stable setup then they led Bryce inside. He seemed completely comfortable.

"Once he's had a little time to get used to being here, I'll bring Midnight by so they can meet before we actually start riding together."

"Sounds good."

"So, what's our plan for the rest of the day?"

"You'll find out."

"What are you up to now?"

"You'll find out."

Alex put her hands on her hips, feigning annoyance, but she loved that Dean had more surprises in store for today. They went inside to grab a light lunch which they took out to her porch to eat, while Holly wandered around sniffing. When they were done, they went inside to clean up.

"My surprise is going to keep us here tonight."

"Okay, then I'll need to grab some stuff, especially if I'll be here overnight."

"You will be."

"Cool! We can drop the trailer off and I'll get what I need for Holly and I."

"Okay."

They headed over to Alex's so she could pack a bag. She unhitched the trailer then they headed back to Dean's house. He carried her bag in and put in the living room. They sat down and watched a little bit of TV before Dean went to the kitchen. He grabbed a few containers out of the fridge and packed a cooler. Alex joined him in the kitchen, bouncing like a kid on Christmas morning.

"Is it time for my surprise?"

"Eager, are we? And yes, baby, let's go. I can't wait until you see tonight's surprise."

"Ooh, yes, I am totally excited. It's absolutely incredible."

"How do you know when it hasn't even happened yet?"

"Because, everything we do together is incredible, so why would this be any less?"

"I aim to please."

"Oh, you definitely do that."

"Come with me, my angel."

They headed down to open area behind his house. Alex's eyes lit up when she saw what he had done. There was a bed, a cooler with food and drinks, one of his guitars and a small table with two chairs. She also saw that he had cleaned up the swimming pool the previous owners installed.

This is amazing. I can't believe you recreated our final night in the Poconos. Does this mean we're going to make love and sleep outside like we did there?"

"In due time, my love, but I have some other activities planned too. Shall we dine?"

Dean put the sandwiches out and took two beers out of the cooler. After they ate and finished their beer, Dean grabbed his guitar and sat down on the bed, motioning for Alex to join him. She sat between his legs, resting her back on his chest. He put the guitar in front of her and began playing. She loved the feeling of his arms around her as he sang a couple of his love songs to her. When he was done playing, Dean flashed Alex a naughty look.

"Baby, it's really warm out here tonight."

Alex watched Dean get up from the bed and remove his clothes and climb into the pool.

"Please join me, my love."

She quickly stripped and walked over to the pool.

"My beautiful goddess, come play in the water with me. I love you."

She loved the way the warm water felt on her bare skin. Dean swam over to her and wrapped his arms around her.

"You're the most beautiful mermaid I've ever seen."

"You're such a dork," Alex said as she playfully splashed him.

Feigning shock, Dean said, "Oooh, you're in trouble now, baby."

Dean pushed her playfully, knocking her on her sexy ass. She pulled him down with her, both of them splashing and laughing like teenagers. Dean stood, helped her up, and embraced her lovingly. Circling her arms around his neck, she pressed her lips to his, sliding her tongue into his mouth eagerly.

"My, my, baby, someone seems a bit horny."

"Oh yes I am. Please take me to that beautiful bed and fuck me. Dean scooped her up in his arms and carried her to the bed. After setting her on her feet, he wrapped her in a towel then wrapped himself so they could dry off before they got into the bed. Alex laid down when she finished drying off.

"I need to feel your hot sexy skin against mine. Please come lay with me, baby."

As soon as he laid down next to her, she got on all fours and wrapped her mouth around his sexy dick. He moaned as she slid her soft lips up and down his shaft, circling her tongue around the tip, while her fingers caressed his balls. The combination of sensations was driving him wild. He slid a couple of fingers inside her, massaging her g-spot as she kept sucking him. She started moaning loudly, the vibrations taking his pleasure up a notch.

"Baby, I want to be inside you."

Alex straddled him, taking him deep inside her. She slowly and sensually slid her pussy up and down his cock, their moaning and breathing in perfect sync. He matched her motion with strong powerful thrusts, sending the most amazing sensations through her whole body. Her breathing became more rapid and she increased her speed, signaling to Dean she was close to an orgasm.

"Baby, go slow, I really want this to last. I love being inside you this way, watching your beautiful body as you fuck me."

Dean wrapped his arms around her and pulled her down on top of him. She lowered her head and kissed him passionately, as he rolled her onto her back. She grabbed his strong muscular arms as she felt him thrusting slowly and deeply.

"Oh, Dean, that feels so good, baby. Please don't stop. Mmmm, oh Dean, oh baby."

Her breathing was becoming heavy again, but this time he didn't slow down and instead, increased his speed until they both exploded together, bodies quaking, covered in sweat, on fire from the passion of their beautiful lovemaking.

Dean looked up at the stars lighting the sky like bright beautiful diamonds. The sight was breathtaking, but did not even come close to the sight of the beautiful woman lying in his arms.

"Baby, I love you more than life itself and I promise I will never leave you. I don't want to know life without you in it, my angel."

"I love you so much, Dean."

He moved back on top of his beautiful woman and spent hours making passionate love to her under the night sky until they were both devoid of energy. After kissing goodnight, they pulled the covers up and drifted off to sleep.

Chapter Eighteen

Dean was awakened the following morning by the sound of his guitar. Looking around, he saw Alex sitting down by the pool, wrapped in a towel, playing. He got up and pulled his jeans on then walked down and sat with her. She stopped playing when she spotted him.

"Baby, why did you stop? You sound amazing. Please, keep playing for me, my queen."

Alex started strumming as she looked over at Dean. She saw him close his eyes, the most blissful look on his face.

After she played a couple more songs, she asked, "What were you just thinking about? You had a really happy look on your face."

"That was from listening to you play. I know you won't believe me, but you truly are talented. I really would love to record some music together when I get my studio done. Of course, I do have to start first," he said laughing.

"And it's because of me that you haven't started. I'm taking up too much of your time."

"Not even close. I have loved spending all this time with you and did so of my own free will. But at some point, I really do need to get started."

"Okay, let's get dressed, grab some breakfast and then get to work!"

"I didn't mean that I was expecting or demanding that you help me."

"I know that. I love doing that kind of work, so please, I want to help you."

"Thank you."

Alex smiled as she headed back to where they left their clothes last night and got dressed. Dean followed suit then they walked up to his house.

"How about a quick bowl of cereal, then we can head over to the studio?"

"Sounds good, as long as I can also get some coffee."

"Of course, breakfast isn't complete without a hot steaming cup of coffee. Or some hot steamy sex," he added with a wink, earning him a playful tap on his bottom.

He smiled at her feistiness as he put on a pot of coffee and gave Alex her cereal choices. After they ate and cleaned up, they showered together then got dressed then headed over to the studio. They got started prepping all the walls to be painted. They moved everything out of the room and taped off what they didn't want to get paint on. Dean showed Alex what walls would be painted what color, so she grabbed a paint can and the tools she needed and got started. He loved seeing her work, watching her sexy body moving around as she painted.

Feeling his eyes on her, she turned around with a stern look on her face.

"Okay, mister, if you don't get your ass to work, you won't get to see my naked ass later."

Pretending to be wounded, Dean lowered his head and got to work, when he suddenly burst out laughing.

"What is so funny?"

"You, baby. You are the sexiest, funniest woman I've ever met. Just hearing you call me mister like that struck me funny for some reason. But now I will get to work. I don't want to miss my chance to see that hot ass in my bed later."

Alex smiled as she turned around to get back to her wall. Several hours later, all the walls were done and the place looked great. Dean was grinning from ear to ear.

"Baby, I love how this turned out. Thank you so much for helping me."

"It was my pleasure. Besides, if I wasn't here bossing you around, you'd still be sitting on your ass," she said, laughing.

Dean feigned shock as he walked over to her and pulled her close, kissing her hard.

"You can be quite mouthy, my love."

"Let me show you just how mouthy."

She put her lips on Dean's neck and started sucking like he'd done to her before, tickling his neck with her tongue. She could feel his dick starting to strain against his jeans.

"Something you like, baby?"

"Hell yeah. I get excited every single time I get near you, especially when your lips are on pretty much any part of my body."

"Mmm, Dean, I think we need to do something about that erection. Let me take to you the couch we moved to the other room and fuck you, my sexy rock star."

Dean's eyes went wide hearing her talk like that. He just about ran to the couch, eager to have his woman wrap her hot body around his. They quickly undressed, both of them boiling over with desire. Dean sat on the couch, smiling as his sexy goddess climbed into his lap and wrapped her hot pussy around his dick. He held her hips as she bounced up and down on his dick hard and fast, both of them climaxing quickly.

"That was incredible. I love our slow, sensual lovemaking, but sometimes a hard, fast fuck feels just as amazing. I love you."

"I love you too. Now that we've satisfied one hunger, how about a lunch break?"

"Sounds good, babe. Let's head up to my house and see what we can come up with."

Alex started looking in his cabinets and found a couple of cans of chicken.

"How does a chicken salad sandwich sound? I've been told I make a mean sandwich."

"That sounds delicious. Anything I can do to help?"

"Just sit there and look sexy, baby," she said with a wink.

Alex explored his kitchen until she found everything she needed.

Once the food was ready, she brought two plates over to the table while Dean grabbed a beer for each of them. He took a bite and realized she wasn't kidding.

"Baby, that's the most delicious chicken salad I've ever had. What's your secret?"

"I'll never tell! Many have tried and all have failed. That secret will die with me."

"I guarantee I can get you to tell me, baby."

Dean walked over to her and started tickling her mercilessly. Alex was doubled over in laughter but she wouldn't spill her secret.

"Is that all you got, Dean? It's going to take a lot more than tickling to get me to give up my recipe."

"Is that a challenge, baby? I hope you know who you're messing with, Alexandra."

With her hands on her hips, she defiantly replied, "I'm not afraid of you."

"I will find out that secret, baby! But right now, I need to take care of something. Can we get together later for some dinner?"

"I would love to."

"Okay, I will head over between 4 and 5. I love you, baby,"

"I love you too, Dean." Dean dropped Alex at home and she headed out to the storage area to get things ready for the upcoming week at the market. She was happy to see she a lot more crops this week, as well eggs. Everyone's been busy, she laughed to herself. She was so grateful for all her help, and especially thankful that they made enough money that she could continue to pay her team even during the reduced hours of wintertime.

After she was done boxing everything up and logging her inventory, Alex headed home to get showered and changed before Dean came over. She wondered what he might have in store for her this time. Certainly there could be no more surprises, she thought to herself. She was wrong! She was just finishing getting dressed when she heard her cell phone ring.

"Hello."

"Hi, beautiful. Are you ready for our date?"

"Almost. I just need to throw my boots on and I will be ready. Do you want me to wait outside?"

"That would be great, baby, See you soon." Alex finished getting ready and headed outside. She stood on her porch waiting to hear the familiar roar of Dean's truck but heard nothing, until suddenly, she heard a sound she knew and loved, the clacking of horseshoes. Her chin dropped to the ground when she saw who was responsible for the sound.

Alex couldn't believe her eyes. The most beautiful white mustang she'd ever seen was standing in front of her, along with a white carriage carrying her prince. He was sporting tight blue jeans, cowboy hat and boots, and a white button-down shirt with the top few buttons open. Alex gawked at him, skin tanned a golden brown, his sexy muscular chest and arms, and that sexy patch of dark hair peeking out of his shirt. Alex couldn't remember how to make words, so she just kept standing there with her mouth hanging open.

"Are you okay?"

"Umm, hello," was all she could muster.

Dean smiled at her reaction.

"I thought we could take a ride. Your chariot, my lady."

Their driver took them on a lap around the town, the first part of the ride lasting about an hour, ending at the park. While the driver gave his horse some food and water, Alex and Dean walked to their favorite bench and sat down. They held hands for a while, just gazing into each others' eyes, completely lost in their love for one another. When they were ready, the headed back to the carriage to finish their tour. The driver took them back to Dean's house when they were done.

"I have something special planned to cook you for dinner tonight, baby. How about we head inside?"

"Sounds yummy."

"Seeing you ride up in that carriage, just about made me pass out. You are easily the sexiest man I have ever seen and I can't wait to get you into bed tonight and ravage you, my sexy prince."

"Mmm, I can't wait, but first I need to thrill you with my cooking. I have a feeling we're going to need quite a bit of energy tonight. The main part of the meal is prepared and just needs to go in the oven. Would you like to help me get the rest of the food ready?"

"Oh yes, I would love to. Just tell me what you need me to do."

"Well, first, I hope you like lasagna."

"Yum, lasagna is one of my favorites."

"Great! I just need to get the salad and garlic bread ready." Alex helped Dean get the rest of the meal ready. I could get used to this, she thought to herself. For the first time in her life, she actually pictured herself being married and living with a man, something that used to scare the hell out of her. She also felt somewhat sad that her father wasn't here to see them rekindle their relationship. Once the lasagna was done baking, they sat down to eat. Dean served them each a plate and poured two glasses of the Moscato they brought home from their Pocono trip.

Alex took a bite of the lasagna.

"Oh my god, this is delicious. This is by far the best lasagna I've ever had."

"Thank you for the compliment. It's so nice to have someone to cook for."

"I agree. I always enjoyed cooking for me and dad, but stopped doing it as much when I was alone. Now, I have a reason to do it more. And for you, I won't limit it to cooking just in the kitchen," she added with that naughty smile he'd grown to love.

After they cleaned up, they went outside and took a walk. Dean took his hand and held hers as they strolled the area around his pool. About halfway around, Dean stopped and pulled her into his muscular arms, kissing her tenderly.

"Baby, I love you so much. Let's finish our walk then head to bed? I really want to make love tonight."

"Mmm, let's go," Alex said eagerly, practically pulled Dean's arm out of its socket.

When they got back inside, they laid down in bed, holding each other. She lovingly ran her hands through his gorgeous black hair, giving him chills. Unlike their past encounters, neither of them took charge and instead, they quietly and tenderly undressed each other as they kissed passionately. As he ran his fingers over her soft skin, he found himself thanking, in his head, the company that made her shower gel. He inhaled deeply, not only loving the feel of her skin, but also the sweet scent of his goddess.

Never breaking their kiss, he gently moved on top of her and entered her more slowly than ever before. Surprisingly to her, his super-slow pace actually felt better than anything she'd felt yet. Words were non-existent, replaced with soft moans from her and deep growls from him as their bodies danced as one. They were truly making love tonight, and it was amazing. The slow, sensual build to the ultimate climax took longer, but was also more intense when they finally reached that magical moment. Quietly, Dean laid next to her and held her lovingly in his strong arms.

"I love you, baby," he whispered softly.

Matching his tone, she caressed his face and said, "I love you too."

They continued silently holding each other as they fell into a deep, peaceful slumber.

Chapter Nineteen

Waking up the next morning after another passionate night, Dean and Alex showered together and ate some breakfast before Dean drove her home.

"Anything on your agenda after we're done at the market today?"

"Nope, all good today, why?"

"Now that the paint is dry, I thought maybe you would want to help me set up the equipment in the studio. Of course, I understand if you don't, so please don't feel pressured."

"Of course I would love to help you."

"Thanks, babe."

They got in Dean's truck and headed to Alex's farm, so they could load up for the market. He noticed she seemed deep in thought as they rode. For a second he got worried she was having second thoughts about being with him, but he pushed that out of his head. He just knew he could never bear losing her again. He barely hung on the first time.

"Something' on your mind?"

"Yeah, I've been thinking about the market."

"What about it?"

"If I want to hire someone to do that full-time so I can spend more time actually at the farm."

"Hmmm, might not be a bad idea," he said in a naughty voice.

"Why?"

"Then you'll have more time to roll in the hay with me."

Alex let loose with that beautiful, melodic laugh he loved so much.

"Well, that definitely makes up my mind."

Once they arrived at the market and got set up, she started working on a flyer to post around the market advertising the job, hoping she might get some takers from the heavy foot traffic passing through the area. She printed off a stack then hung one on the counter at her stall. Dean took the rest and walked around the market, hanging them up in all the highest traffic areas. When he was done, he grabbed two coffees and two cheese danishes and headed back to Alex.

"Thanks. I love danish and you know coffee is my potion of choice."

"Any time, babe."

Lunch time was here before they knew it. Alex closed the stand so they could head down to the food court and enjoy lunch together. They bumped into Hannah, so the three of them ate together.

Alex asked, "How's the stand doing so far?"

"Amazing. Thank you so much. I'm actually going to hire someone to run it so I can get back to the store."

"Funny you say that, I just had Dean put up fliers today for a job at my stand so I can spend more time at the farm."

"I would too if my boyfriend was a rock star," Hannah said teasingly.

Alex looked over at Dean and smiled wide. She really was lucky.

Hannah continued, "Honestly, at this point, I would date just about anyone. It's been quite the dry spell."

"I find that hard to believe, my adorable friend."

"Thanks."

Dean didn't interject, but he knew someone who would be perfect for Hannah. Too bad he lived in LA. Once they finished lunch, they headed back to their booths to finish out their day. Just as Alex was getting ready to pack up for the day, she had a woman approach her with a small child in tow.

"Hello, how can I help you?"

"I saw your flier and was interested in the job. Before I waste your time though, could I ask you something?"

"Of course."

"Would I be required to find child care?"

Alex could tell by the tone in her voice having to find childcare would mean she couldn't take the job. As there were no specific rules, other than Alex needing to add some extra insurance, she decided she would allow it.

"As long as having your child here wouldn't interfere with you performing your required duties, I have no problem with it. Would you be available to come back tomorrow for an interview?"

"Oh yes, thank you. What time?"

"You tell me what works with your schedule?"

"This little one always has me up early."

"Does 9 work?"

"Yes, I'll be here and thank you again so much. You have no idea what this means to me."

"I look forward to chatting with you tomorrow."

Alex finished packing up then she and Dean carried her stuff out to his truck.

"So, if you end up hiring her, what does that mean for us?"

"Anything you want."

'Hmmm..."

"Oh, yeah, plenty of that."

They grabbed a pizza on the way home so they could get right to the studio and get to work. Whey got inside, she was surprised to see the work was all done.

"I thought you wanted me to help you get set up."

"That was a trick to get you here!"

"You never have to trick me."

"I know but I have a special surprise and I didn't want to give that away."

"Oooh, when can I see it?"

"After we eat."

"Okay."

After they each ate a couple of slices and downed a beer, Alex started bouncing in her chair. Dean was laughing at her reaction, knowing full well she was dying to see her surprise.

"Well, are ya ready, babe?"

"Oh my god, yes," she squealed.

"Come with me."

Dean led Alex down to the end of the hall to a locked door covered with a painter's tarp. He removed the tarp and she couldn't believe her eyes. Painted on the door was 'The Love Nest,' along with two inter-twined hearts. Dean was painted on one heart, Alexandra on the other.

Pointing at the door, she said, "I love this."

"Wait until you see the inside!"

He unlocked the door and they walked in. Dean turned the light on and for the second time tonight, Alex couldn't believe her eyes. She saw a beautiful heart shaped tub in the corner and a king-sized bed on the far side of the room. There was a large, flat screen TV mounted on the wall opposite of the bed. There was also a couch and a desk in the room. She looked and saw one more door off the side.

"What's behind that door?"

"Open it."

Behind that door was a smaller side room, with a dog bed, food and water bowls, and a bunch of toys.

"You made Holly her own little room!"

"Of course, she's my other girl!"

"This is amazing!"

"I wanted a place close to home that we could use as an escape for songwriting, relaxing, well, anything your heart desires."

"Or anything my body desires."

"Of course."

"Then get your clothes off. Now!"

Dean got up and quickly did as she commanded.

"Good. Now park that hot ass on the couch and..."

Alex stopped herself before finishing her next instruction, her face turned a bright crimson.

"What, baby?"

"I can't."

"Baby, tell me what you're fantasizing."

Suddenly finding some courage, Alex looked Dean straight in his eyes and said, "I want to watch you stroke your own dick."

Not breaking eye contact, he did as she asked. He watched her licking her lips as she watched him.

"Damn, that's hot, but now it's my turn."

Alex walked over, got on her knees and wrapped her sexy mouth around his dick, sucking and licking hard. Dean threw his head back and groaned as his hot lover sucked off his rock hard erection. When she couldn't stand not having him inside her any longer, she stood and quickly got naked herself then returned to the couch.

She lowered herself onto Dean's lap, taking his dick inside her. She was so wet, he slid in easily. Pressing her incredible breasts against his sexy chest, she fucked him hard and fast until they both exploded. She loved the feeling of his dick inside her more than anything else she'd ever felt and couldn't get enough of being naked with her sexy man.

"Fuck, so fuckin' good. Now it's my turn to instruct you."

"Bring it, stud."

"Couch, now!"

Alex sat down, her breathing increasing with excitement as she waited for his next command.

"Spread those sexy legs baby. I wanna see that sweet pussy."

Alex opened her legs and the feeling of being on display turned her on more than she thought it would, and a moan escaped her lips.

"So good, baby. Now, I wanna see your fingers inside your hot pussy."

Alex blushed and hesitated for a minute.

"Now, baby! I am dying to see your sexy fingers rubbing your hot clit."

Alex took a deep breath, and started teasing her own pussy. She moaned with pleasure as she got herself off while Dean watched her. She knew she was getting him hot when she saw his cock get hard. She started imagining it was him touching her and she rubbed harder, her moaning increasing.

"Fuck, I want you, woman. Lay down for me so I can fuck that sweet pussy."

Alex laid back on the couch and Dean laid on top of her, propping himself up so she didn't bear his full weight. She moaned loudly when she felt his sexy cock. She grabbed his ass, pushing him in harder and deeper as he fucked her. After watching her pleasure herself, he was close to the edge and quickly filled her pussy with his cum, before he could bring her to orgasm.

"Wow, Dean, you must have really liked the show I gave you."

Dean smiled and commanded, "I wanna see your hot naked body on the desk now!"

Alex walked over and sat on the desk. Dean spread her legs wide and jammed his tongue eagerly into her sweet pussy, licking and sucking until her entire body shook with pleasure. She threw her head back and screamed at the pleasure. Instead of stopping, Dean kept licking and sucking her clit as he slid a couple fingers inside her. He brought her to orgasm after orgasm, each one more intense than the one before it until she was screaming at the top of her lungs.

"Oh god, oh Dean, I can't take it anymore, oh fuck, please, holy shit."

Dean ignore her and kept licking and sucking her, as her body quivered harder and harder. The pleasure was more intense than anything she'd ever felt. Her entire body was on fire and she completely forgot where she was, even who she with how incredible he was making her feel. He got so turned on that again his dick was hard. He slid inside her slowly.

"Baby, tell me how that feels."

"I'm so sensitive after all those orgasms that even the slightest move is sending me into space. Please keep fucking me slow, it's so good."

Dean fucked her slower than ever before, each stroke feeling like she was floating. Her pussy was on fire and she felt like she was close to squirting like she did the other day. She lifted her hips trying to get the angle she needed to have Dean's dick hit her g-spot. After a few more slow but powerful thrusts, she felt her dam burst, soaking Dean's dick with her love juice. Her incredible orgasm sent him over the edge and he filled her with his salty delicious cream.

"Fuck, baby, that was incredible."

"Mmm, yes it was, baby."

"I guess we should get some sleep."

"Okay, but could we do one little thing first?"

"What?"

"A nice soak in that amazing tub you installed."

"That sounds like just what we both need, my angel."

Dean lowered the lights before they got in the tub. The warm water and massage jets left them both feeling relaxed and sleepy. Once they got out, they were too tired to even go back to the house, so they decided to sleep in the bed Dean put in their getaway room. Holly curled up on her bed and quickly fell fast asleep. The minute he turned out the light, they kissed goodnight and were out cold.

The next morning, they had some breakfast together then headed over to Alex's to grab what she needed for the market and take Holly home. Alex would hopefully be hiring someone to take over running the stand. She was looking forward to the chance to spend more time at the farm and of course, more time in Dean's sexy arms. At about 8:45, Alex saw the woman she spoke with yesterday. The fact that she was early already gave her some bonus points. Alex took her in the back office while Dean took care of the stand.

"I apologize for not asking this yesterday, but could you tell me your name?"

"Andrea Jones."

"Alex Peterson. It's nice to properly make your acquaintance."

After reviewing Andrea's work history, Alex knew she would be perfect. She just had one last question, always an important one to her when making hiring decisions.

"Can you tell me why you left your last job, after so many years?"

"I had a tough pregnancy and needed extra time off before I delivered. My previous employer wouldn't grant me a leave of absence, so I had no choice."

"I'm so sorry, That won't be an issue any longer. I just need a couple of moments to prepare your offer letter, if you can sit tight?"

A bright smile swept across Andrea's face as she said, "Of course."

Alex returned from her computer after printing off copies of the letter. She presented Andrea with salary and benefit information. Andrea accepted the position and would begin the following morning. Alex would have one of her team train Andrea, as well as take care of delivering the produce to the market every morning. She walked Andrea out, let her know what time to arrive in the morning, and let her know what she needed to bring with her. Once Andrea headed out, she gave Dean a big hug, so happy to have the position filled that fast. Once they had finished up for the day, they headed home and treated themselves to a night of cereal eating and TV binging before they headed of to bed.

Chapter Twenty

Alex got up the next morning, got ready and headed down to the market to complete Andrea's paperwork and turn her over to a member of her staff to train. While she was gone, Dean was busy cooking up yet another surprise for her. This one though was a whole new level and he had to admit, nerves were starting to kick in as he drove over to Chris's house. When he arrived, Chris and Tracey greeted him with an excited hug.

"Thanks for agreeing to watch Holly."

"Of course, the girls love her and they're excited. Dude, we're so happy for you," Chris said as he handed Dean the ring box.

Tracey nodded in agreement, tears filling her eyes. She gave Dean another hug then went back inside.

"What if she says no?"

"Man, come on. That woman loves you."

"I'm nervous."

"I get it. Just breathe. You'll be fine. One piece of advice. Never take your eyes off her face. I saw Tracey's reaction when I asked her and it's something I'll never forget."

"Thanks for everything, man."

Dean got back in his truck as he had a few more things to grab and he wanted to make sure he beat Alex home. This would be a trip she would never forget. He got home and was happy to see Alex was still at the market. He packed up his clothes then pack a second bag with his surprises, including that magical velvet box. He did his best to keep his nerves at bay. Alex got back to Dean's about half an hour later and found him sitting on the porch.

"Baby, do you have enough clothes here for a couple days or do you need more?"

"I have enough, why?"

"Go pack a bag."

"Why?"

"I'm taking you to Ocean City for a couple of days. Maryland, not Jersey."

"A beach trip sounds perfect."

"Oh it will be."

Now what did that man have up his sleeve? She could only imagine but she had a feeling she would love it. She quickly got her stuff together and loaded into his truck and they headed out. She was so excited as the beach was one of her favorite getaway spots. Her dad had always loved the beach too, so he made sure they spent plenty of time there. Dean looked over at her, and noticed she was lost in her thoughts.

"Whatcha thinkin' about, babe?"

"My dad. He always loved taking me to the beach. I'm so grateful to have those memories of him."

"I wish he was still here."

"Me too. Hopefully, we'll see him today."

"What do you mean?"

"I never told anyone the last thing he said to me right before he passed, because it was so personal, but I want to tell you."

"Please. I would love to hear it."

"He told me that any time I missed him or felt alone, to look up at the sky. If I saw a red-tailed hawk fly over, that was him. He found them to be so majestic and so powerful and he loved watching them soar through the sky."

"I love that so much. Thank you for sharing something so personal."

Dean reached over and tenderly touched Alex's hand. A minute later, he heard her gasp.

"Are you okay?"

Alex pointed at the sky. Dean couldn't believe his eyes when he saw a beautiful red-tailed hawk flying alongside his truck. Alex had tears streaming down her cheeks. The moment was so powerful, that Dean felt his own eyes well up with tears. He found a spot to pull over. They both got out and stood together watching until the hawk soared out of sight.

"I love you, daddy."

Dean wrapped his arms around her as she wept. All of his nerves about the proposal melted away. He felt like her dad was sending the message that he approved. He really wanted to tell Alex that, but he didn't want to risk spoiling his surprise for later. A few minutes later, Alex lifted her head and as she gazed into Dean's eyes, she kissed him softly.

"Thank you for being here with me at this moment. I know for sure that was my dad giving me a sign that he approves of you being my man."

They got back in the truck and finished the drive to the beach. Dean headed to the house he rented. After unloading their stuff, they went to the boardwalk to grab some lunch then took a nice, relaxing dip in the ocean. The water temperature was perfect as was the weather. The sky was a bright blue with not a cloud in sight, and the temperature was a comfortable 75 with no humidity. He couldn't have asked for a more perfect day, but he was even more excited about what the night would bring. When they were done, they went back to the rental house to shower and change for dinner. Dean wouldn't give her even the slightest hint of their plans for the evening.

Dean made her wait in the bedroom with the door shut while he got everything ready. He had a bouquet of her favorite Gerbera daisies, a picnic dinner, wine, romantic music, and of course a little velvet box, which he tucked in his pocket. Once he had everything packed up, he went into the bedroom to let her know he was ready. They walked to a roped off part of the beach. Inside the roped off area was a small table with two chairs.

"Your table, my lady," Dean said in a fake British accent as he lifted the rope.

"Thank you, my lord."

He walked her to the table and pulled her chair out for her. After she sat, he sat across from her and opened the bag he had been carrying, pulling out two bowls of chicken Caesar salad he made along with a bottle of wine and two glasses. After they finished eating, he pulled the bouquet of daisies out and handed them to her, earning him that beautiful smile he loved so much.

"Thank you, they're beautiful."

"Just like the woman holding them."

He pulled his MP3 player out of the bag and put some romantic music on. The sun had finished its descent and they were left with just the light of the beautiful full moon that out tonight. Suddenly, Dean stood and walked over to where she was sitting. He moved the table off to the side. While gazing into her eyes, he took her hands in his.

"Alexandra, when I first met you, I fell in love with you. I made a terrible mistake choosing my career over our love. I am so very thankful that you were willing to give me another chance all these years later. I promise you I will never make that same mistake again. I want to spend the rest of my days on this earth loving you."

Dean got down on one knee and reached into his pocket, pulling out a beautiful velvet box. Alex gasped as tears filled her eyes.

"Baby, will you marry me?"

"Oh, Dean, yes of course I will marry you."

He pulled the ring out and placed it on her finger as tears spilled out of her eyes. He stood, helped her to her feet and pulled her into a tight embrace. She felt his lips tenderly caress hers, their tongues twirling together in a passionate kiss. As they were kissing, they heard a loud screech from above. Looking up, they saw a red-tailed hawk fly over. Tears filled their eyes as they watched the hawk circling overhead several times before flying away.

"I think it's safe to say my father approves."

Dean kissed her tenderly. They danced together for several songs.

"Dean, can we head back to the house now?"

"Sure, why?"

"I need to feel you make love to me."

Dean grabbed the bag while Alex picked up her bouquet and they walked back to the house. Once they were inside, Dean scooped her up and carried her over to the bed, gently laying her down. He laid next to her and kissed her passionately as he slid his hands under her shirt, caressing her silky skin. He lifted her shirt off and removed her bra, running his tongue over her beautiful breasts. Alex stripped Dean of his shirt and pulled him close, loving the feeling of his sexy chest against hers. Dean unbuttoned her jeans, and slowly slid the zipper down, tickling her with his fingers. After removing her sneakers and socks, he removed her jeans followed by her panties, caressing her skin as he did.

Alex moaned as Dean spread he legs and slid a couple fingers inside her. She moaned even louder as Dean stroked her clit. He slid his fingers out, slid his body down and replaced them with his tongue. He ran his tongue up and down her pussy, stopping to suck on her clit. Fuck, she tasted so good. He licked her clit hard, sliding his fingers back inside her, stroking her g-spot hard.

"Oh Dean, so good. Please don't stop, oh fuck."

He kept going until her entire body was shaking with a powerful climax. He again laid next to her and felt Alex reach her hands out and open his jeans, sliding her hand down his underpants and stroking his hard cock as he groaned at her soft touch. Dean stood up, removed the rest of his clothes and laid back down. Alex got on all fours and wrapped her soft mouth around his balls, sucking gently. She moved to his dick, sliding her lips up and down, swirling her tongue around the tip like a delicious ice cream cone.

"So fuckin' good, baby."

"Mmmm. I want that hot cock inside my pussy. Please, baby."

"On your back. Now."

Alex laid on her back, smiling as Dean climbed on top of her and slid his dick deep inside her. He lifted her sexy ass with his hands so he could plunge deeper into her hot, wet pussy. Fuck, she felt so good. His thrusts were slow and deliberate, building the pressure inside her. Dean lowered her ass back down, and wrapped his arms around her, kissing her passionately, his tongue exploring her mouth as they continued their passionate dance for a gloriously long time, celebrating their engagement, their love, the joining of bodies and souls until the pressure reached its breaking point. Like birds taking flight, they soared through the night skies, fueled only by their ecstasy, riding wave after wave of intense pleasure.

"Dean, that was incredible as always, but something felt different this time."

"Different better or different worse?"

"Definitely better."

"I agree. You made me the happiest man alive when you accepted my proposal. More than any other time we've been together, we truly made love, Alexandra."

"Oh, please tell me it will only keep getting better."

"Oh yes, baby, I promise you that. I cannot wait to tell the world that you're going to be my wife. I love you."

"I love you too. I love you so much that I want to spend the rest of the night right here, making love until the sun awakens."

Before he could respond, she pushed him onto his back and mounted him but without taking him inside her. She pressed her chest down on his, kissing him even more passionately than he had her. She ran her hands up and down his muscular body, feeling his erection grow against her. Still, she didn't take him inside, which left him writhing in anticipation.

"Baby, take me inside you."

Flashing him his favorite naughty look, she responded, "In due time, my love."

She worked her way down his body, showering his neck, his chest and his abs with her soft kisses. She slid her body down, and started sucking the insides of his thighs, one then the other. She was so close to his dick that it was driving him crazy not to be inside her. She moved her up slightly and took his dick into her mouth. She took every last inch inside her mouth, the sexiest thing he'd ever seen. She was the only woman who'd ever been able to handle his massive length and it was so fucking hot, he thought he might shoot his load.

"Fuck, baby, nobody's ever been able to that to me but you, taking my entire dick."

"You taste so fucking good. Please let me drink your delicious cream."

"Oh god," was all he could manage before she felt her mouth fill with his cream.

She sat up, looking deep into his eyes and swallowed every last delicious drop, licking her lips when she was done. Watching her drink him down activated his launch sequence. She looked down at his dick, smiled, and wrapped her wet pussy around him, sliding up and down his shaft. He matched her with powerful thrusts of his own until again their bodies took flight, like two rockets blasting off into outer space.

They spent the rest of the night in each others' arms making love over and over until they were completely spent. Dean pulled the covers over them and they laid together, watching the sun make its appearance over the horizon. They slept until almost noon then packed up to head back home. After stopping by Chris's to pick up Holly and get huge excited hugs of congratulations, they headed back to Dean's house. After unloading his truck, they carried everything inside. Dean walked over to her, hands on his hips.

"Alexandra, the bedroom. Now!"

She quickly walked to his bedroom, as he followed close behind her. As soon as they were inside her bedroom, Dean walked over and sat down on the bed.

"Strip for me now! Slowly!"

Alex felt that familiar heat between her legs. She made eye contact with Dean, teasingly licked her lips and slowly lifted her shirt over her head, letting it drop to the floor. Dean growled as he saw her sexy skin, growling louder as she removed her bra, exposing her amazing breasts. She turned her back to him and bent down to remove her boots and socks, giving him a view of her perfect ass. Facing him again, she removed her jeans and panties. Her naked body was met with a loud whistle as Dean got up and took her into his arms.

"Mmmm, I've missed this skin. Lay down and wait for me, baby."

"You've missed my skin? It hasn't been that long."

"Even five seconds leaves me missing your naked body."

Dean quickly removed his clothing and laid down next to Alex. He spread her legs, exposing her beautiful pussy and slid a couple of fingers inside her. She moaned as she ground against his fingers, heat quickly spreading over her entire body. She reached her arms out and wrapped them around her lover, never wanting to let him go again. She ran her fingers through his hair as he kept pleasuring her with his magic fingers.

"I love you, Dean."

"Love you."

Dean kissed her hard as he moved his body on top of hers, sliding his dick inside her. Slowly and sensually, he moved in and out of her with the passion she'd grown to love. The more excited he felt her get, the more he slowed his pace. Dean wanted this to last, wanted her to never again experience life without him. He growled when he felt her nails raking his back, growled even louder when her hands moved down to his ass. He felt her hands massaging his ass hard as he fucked her pussy until he couldn't hold back. His dick exploded like a volcano, filling her pussy with his hot lava.

He laid next to her and spread her legs wider. She moaned loudly as he massaged her clit with his fingers.

"So good, oh, harder, please, baby."

Dean increased the power and speed of his fingers as she writhed and screamed with pleasure. She felt the pressure reach a boiling point. Her body took flight, soaring through the sun-filled sky as wave after wave of pleasure left her feeling like she was floating on a cloud. She sighed with contentment as she collapsed her body against his, the feeling of his hot skin exciting her so much that she grabbed his dick, stroking it until she felt him get hard again.

Alex pushed Dean on his back and mounted him. She wrapped her pussy, still slick from his cream and her orgasm, and took his dick deep inside. Using his hard, muscular quads for balance, she bounced up and down fast and hard. Fuck, he felt so damn good inside her. Dean felt himself getting close to another explosion and wanted her to slow down.

"Please, baby, go slower. I want to enjoy every single second of you fucking me."

Alex slowed down her pace, making each stroke up and down his cock take an amazingly long time. He put his hands on her sexy stomach and ran them up to her amazing tits, working her nipples between his fingers until they were as hard as diamonds. Alex slid her hands down his thighs so she could lean her body back, the angle stimulating her g-spot with an intensity unlike anything she'd ever felt. Dean moved his hands south, using his fingers to stimulate her clit while she rode him. The combination of everything shot her into another galaxy.

"Holy fuck, that feels so fucking good. Oh fuck, oh Dean. Mmm, baby, fuck, so good."

"Alexandra, my love, being inside you is the most incredible thing I've ever felt."

Dean exploded inside her once again, filling her with that hot man-juice she loved so much. She collapsed her chest onto Dean's, both of breathing hard and drenched in sweat. The beautiful aroma of love and sex filled the room, leaving them both in a blissful trance. Alex laid down next to Dean and nestled herself into those strong, muscular arms she loved so much.

Alex heard her stomach growl and turned beet red in the face. Dean tried to stifle a laugh but couldn't.

"I'm starving too. How about we grab a shower together then go out and celebrate our engagement?"

"Now why would you think I'd want to stand naked with you in a hot, steamy shower?"

Dean pulled her close, his hands on her ass, and kissed her passionately.

"Yep, that's why," she added breathlessly.

Holding hands, they walked down to Alex's bathroom and got in the shower together. The hot water felt amazing cascading down their naked bodies, pressed together in a passionate embrace, exploring each others' mouths with their tongues. After the finished showering and getting dressed, they headed out to dinner.

Dean asked, "Where do you wanna eat?"

"I have a perfect idea. Let's go to the diner we ate at the night we met. I think it seems the perfect place to celebrate our engagement."

'I love it. Let's go."

They got to the diner and ordered coffee along with the same break-fast they ordered that night. They laughed and talked just like they used to, only this time, she had a beautiful diamond on her finger. Part of her still couldn't believe this was actually happening, but here she was, sitting across the table from the sexiest man she'd ever know. Once they were done eating, they headed back to Dean's.

"Glad you picked there. It was great! I love you."

"I love you. Now, take me back to you house and fuck my brains out."

Dean almost ran off the road when he heard her say that.

"My, my, you sure are being naughty tonight, baby."

"You ain't seen nothin' yet, sexy."

Dean mashed the gas pedal to the floor!

Chapter Twenty-One

"I think that was the fastest I've seen you get home!"

"Baby, I want you so fuckin' bad. My bedroom now!"

They raced inside and practically knocked each other down trying to get to the bedroom. Alex stood, hands on her hips, stern look on her face.

"What, baby?"

"Strip! Now! Slowly!"

Dean removed his clothes as she commanded. Alex licked her lips sensually as more and more of his skin appeared. She looked down and saw his huge cock was fully erect.

"Damn, babe, look at that fuckin' sexy cock. I need to come play with that. On your back! Now!"

Dean loved when she was like this. He laid down and waited anxiously for what she had in mind. She didn't move for what felt like forever. He was writhing on the bed, wanting to feel her hands, her lips, her anything at this point.

"Fuck, you're killing me."

Alex flashed him the naughtiest look he'd ever seen. If possible, his dick got even harder. He wanted her so bad, he was aching. Alex removed her sneakers and socks, but left the rest of her clothing on. She climbed onto the bed and crawled over to him. Just when he thought he'd seen her do the sexiest damn thing ever, she took it up a notch. Alex straddled him, making eye contact as she again licked her lips, earning a low growl from her sexy tiger. His groans increased in volume as she lowered her head and wrapped her soft lips around his erection. As she continued sucking his massive dick, she ran her hands all over his sexy abs. He couldn't hold back and filled her mouth with a load of his delicious cream. Alex lifted her head and swallowed every last drop.

Alex got off the bed and grabbed her phone, putting on one of those dirty rock songs they both loved. She started swaying her hips in the sexiest dance Dean had ever seen. As she moved to the music, she performed the hottest striptease he'd ever seen, getting him hard as a rock again. When the song ended, his beautiful naked goddess laid down next to him.

In that sexy voice he loved so much, he heard her say, "Baby, fuck me now. I need that cock inside me."

Dean moved on top of his lover and thrust his dick as deep inside her pussy as he could, his balls slapping her sexy ass. She moaned loudly as he filled her with his huge erection.

"Oh Dean, so good. Fuck me harder. Oh, baby, so fucking incredible."

Dean fucked her hard and fast until they both exploded in orgasms so strong and so intense the bed was banging into the wall as their bodies quivered with more power than an earthquake. Dean moved next to her and held her tight, both of their chests heaving and bodies glistening with sweat from their pleasure-filled workout.

"You're so damn hot, woman."

"Mmmm, so are you."

Alex reached down between his legs, lightly running her fingers over his balls and boom he was hard again. She mounted her sexy man, taking his dick inside her again. She laid her chest on his as she slid up and down his hot manhood.

Looking into Dean's eyes, she said, "I'm being a very naughty girl tonight. I think you need to punish me. Please, baby, spank my ass while I keep fucking that huge cock."

Alex moaned as she felt Dean's hands softly make contact with her ass.

"Mmm, harder baby."

Dean's eyes went wide for a second, surprised by her words. He recovered and spanked her a little harder. Fuck, this woman is like no other, he thought.

"Don't stop. Please keep punishing me. It feels so fucking good."

Dean spanked her as she kept that hot wet pussy wrapped around his dick. She sat up straight, taking him in deeper than ever before, her sexy tits bouncing like crazy. She angled her body so that her g-spot was rubbing against his dick. She rocked him harder and harder, screaming with pleasure when suddenly Dean felt warm liquid cover his dick. Alex's entire body was shaking as she squirted her sex juice all over his dick. Watching and feeling her experience that powerful of an orgasm sent him over the edge and he again filled that hot pussy with his cum.

"OH FUCK, DEAN!"

"That was so fucking hot, my goddess."

Alex was so drained of energy she could barely climb off, but she managed to lay next to him. She nestled her head on his chest as he lovingly stroked her hair. She let out a contented sigh then drifted off to sleep. Not wanting to wake her, he just held her, gazing at his sleeping angel. He was filled with so much love for her, he thought his heart would burst. She stirred a little while later.

Sleepily, she whispered, "I need a shower."

After a quick shower, they climbed into bed, still naked and fell asleep in each others' arms, both of them eager to see what tomorrow would bring. They awakened completely refreshed from a great night's, both of them famished from their night of passion. They headed down to Dean's kitchen and prepared breakfast together. She loved preparing meals together, something they'd be able to do for the rest of their lives.

Looking distracted, Dean said, "Babe, I need to ask you somethin'."

"What?"

"Whose house are we going to live in?"

"Hmmm, I hadn't thought about that."

"I was thinking your house, only so you can keep an eye on your business."

"Thank you."

"Of course."

"I'm excited to have you move in. I have plenty of space for your stuff."

"Cool. Wanna go get some boxes today?"

"Eager are we?"

"I never want to spend another night without my goddess."

"Okay. I just want to make a quick stop and check on Andrea."

As expected, Andrea was doing amazing, and all the customers loved her. They headed off in search of boxes and as they were driving, Dean turned down an all-too-familiar driveway.

"I think we need to tell George and Margie the good news."

"Yes we do!"

George called to Margie when he saw Alex and Dean get out of the truck. Alex had her hand in her pocket, hiding their surprise. When Margie came outside, Alex pulled her hand out and showed them her ring. They pulled her and Dean into a huge hug, excitedly congratulating them. Margie had tears streaming down her face and it was clear how much she loved Alex.

"George, I need to ask a huge favor of you."

"Anything, sweetheart."

"My father respected you more than pretty much anyone else he'd ever met, so I know he would approve of this. Will you do me the honor of walking me down the aisle?"

"It'll be my honor."

"Thank you. We haven't talked about any plans yet, but we'll be in touch when we do. Right now, we're off to grab some boxes so Dean can start getting packed to move into my farm."

George and Margie stood with huge smiles on their face as they watched Dean and Alex head out. They went down to the local moving company and got what they needed then headed to Dean's to start packing up some stuff.

"I figured I would start with clothes and toiletries. The rest we can decide on later, especially the furniture."

Once they were done with what he wanted to get packed today, they loaded everything in the truck. As they were pulling out of his driveway, he noticed they weren't alone. A red-tailed hawk followed them all the way to Alex's house. The hawk hovered overhead as they walked to Alex's porch then disappeared over the horizon. Once the hawk was out of sight, they went inside and spent the rest of the afternoon unpacking his boxes and getting everything put away.

"I thought maybe we could go grab some sandwiches for dinner," she said.

"Sounds good."

They ran down to their favorite sandwich shop to grab the food.

"I would love to eat outside and enjoy the beautiful weather this evening."

"Cool," he responded.

"Then afterwards, maybe a repeat of last night?"

"Sex?"

"Duh!"

"Stop being naughty or else!"

"But, Dean..."

Alex never got to finish that sentence. Dean crushed his lips to hers and kissed her hard, jamming his tongue in her mouth. She twirled her tongue around his, her panties soaked with the anticipation of being naked in his arms later. Damn this man does things to me, she thought naughtily. After they came up for air, they walked down to the pond and enjoyed dinner together. They laid back in the grass when they were done eating, gazing up at the beautiful blue sky. They laid there holding each other and kissing until they were both so horny, they couldn't wait another second to get naked. Practically running back to Alex's house, they raced to her bedroom and eagerly stripped each other naked.

They laid down in bed and hugged each other tightly. Alex crushed her lips to Dean's, her tongue eagerly making love to his. She could feel his erection growing against her leg as she felt her favorite warmth spread though her body, her pussy dripping wet with desire. When they finally came up for air, chests heaving, Alex flashed Dean a naughty look.

"Baby, fuck me from behind."

She got on all fours, waiting to feel his cock inside her. Dean whistled when he saw her sexy ass right in front of him. She felt Dean climb onto the bed behind her, put his hands on her hips and press his body against hers. She gasped when she felt his huge dick slide deep inside her pussy, as he moved one hand to her clit. Dean rocked his lower body back and forth, sliding his dick in and out of her sweet pussy. She could feel his sexy balls slapping her pussy with every powerful thrust, as the sounds of her moans and his growls shattering the silence.

"Baby, relax your arms so your body angles downward."

Alex did as he asked. The angle of her body allowed him to fuck her even deeper, stimulating her g-spot with more intensity than ever before. Dean stroked her clit with his strong, masterful fingers. The delicious cocktail of pleasures he was mixing for her left her drunk with passion, her body feeling like she was floating through space.

"Oh fuck, baby, so good. Holy shit, baby. I'm coming, oh god, oh Dean. Aaahh."

Warm liquid gushed from her pussy as she exploded with an intensity equal to a fireworks finale. Screaming with ecstasy as her sweat-covered body shook like a 10.0 earthquake.

"Fuck, Alex, that was so damn sexy. Oh fuck," he growled as he filled her pussy with his lava.

"Oh, Dean, just when I thought I had felt the most intense orgasm of my life, you turn it up ten notches. So fucking good."

"Baby, you're so fuckin' sexy. Look what you did to my dick."

"Damn, fuckin' rock hard again."

He wrapped his arms around her waist and flipped them over so they were in reverse-cowgirl. She took his dick inside her as he lifted her up and down his erection with his strong hands. She leaned forward, grinding her clit against his manhood, moaning loudly as she moved ever closer to another powerful climax.

"Oh, Dean, I love you so much."

"I love you, baby."

They were again one heart, one mind, one soul and now one body, as they climaxed together in a more subdued, but also more passionate and loving orgasm. She slid her body off his, lying next to him, her head on his chest.

"Baby, this is our house now, our bed, our everything."

"Mmmm. I'm the happiest I've ever been."

"Me too, my sexy man."

They held each other tight, making love until the sun's rays streamed through their windows then drifted off to a couple of blissful hours of sleep.

Chapter Twenty-Two

They woke up the next morning and started talking wedding plans over breakfast. They settled on a date then went to the county courthouse to apply for their marriage license. Alex still had a small fear that she was going to wake up and find this was all a dream, but it sure as hell seemed real.

"Where do you wanna have the ceremony?"

"How about here, my goddess?"

"I love that idea."

"Does the date give you enough time?"

"Yep. I don't want a fancy dress or anything. I'm having lunch with the girls today, to tell them we're engaged so now I'll have more to tell them."

"I gotta couple calls to make while you're out,"

"Who?"

"Need to tell Chris the date, then I have a few friends from LA that I want to fly out to be groomsmen."

"Cool! I'm gonna ask the girls, but I'm making them all matrons of honor since I adore all four of them."

They headed down to the courthouse completed their application. Pennsylvania has a 72 hour waiting period, so they would be notified when to come back and pick up the license. As they were heading home, they saw Chris's car at the dog park and they pulled in. Chris and the girls were there with Daisy. Alex went to play with them while Dean sat down to talk to Chris.

"Hey man, no Tracey?"

"She took her mom shopping this morning."

"We were heading home from the courthouse and saw your car."

"Courthouse?"

"Marriage license."

"Dude!"

"We set our date."

"When?"

"One month from today."

"Awesome."

He looked out at Alex, running and laughing with his kids and dog and continued, "Dude, she's amazing."

"You don't have to tell me."

"Truth, while they're out of earshot. Is she still as hot in bed?"

"Hotter and dirtier."

Dean couldn't give any more details as the girls were heading back. Alex looked back and forth at their faces and she knew they'd been talking about her.

"Busted, guys," she said, laughing. "Lucky for you, I find it flattering."

They all headed out to their cars together and said their goodbyes. Alex told Chris she'd love to have the girls be part of the wedding and that she'd call Tracey to talk. As they were riding home, Alex had to know what they'd been talking about.

"So, what did you tell him?"

"Bro code, babe."

"Guess I'll have to get it out you later."

"Is that a challenge?"

"One that I fully intend to win."

"We'll see!"

They laughed the rest of the way home. Alex knew all she'd have to do is get naked and he'd tell her! And, getting naked definitely had quite a few other perks. When they got back to the house, she grabbed a quick shower and got ready to meet the girls for lunch. She was so excited to share her news that she was the first one there. She was waiting at their favorite table when everyone else arrived, making sure she kept her hand hidden. Once they were all seated, she sat there with the biggest smile on her face.

Dee asked, "What's with the shit eatin' grin?"

Alex took her hand out of her pocket and showed them. Everyone else in the restaurant turned to stare when they heard four women cheering very loudly. They all got up and shared a hug before they ordered pizza and wine to celebrate.

"There's one more thing, girls. I would like all of you to be my matrons of honor."

All five of them were sitting in tears as they all agreed. They were all so happy that Alex had finally found that special someone. They spent the next several hours eating, drinking, laughing and talking. She loved these women and was so lucky to have them in her life. Once they were done, Alex headed back home. Just the thought of Dean being there waiting her was getting her excited, especially after a couple of glasses of wine!

It was a warmer day outside, so when she got home, she found him sitting on the porch shirtless, and almost crashed her car. He was so damn sexy. She walked up to him and without so much as a hello, crushed her lips to his, jammed her tongue in his mouth and ran her fingers all over his chest. Feeling especially naughty, she opened his jeans right there on the porch, ecstatic to find he wasn't wearing any underwear.

"Inside. NOW!"

There was a hunger in her eyes like nothing he'd ever seen before and he quickly flew into the house. She didn't even wait until they were in the bedroom and she was on her knees, mouth wrapped around his cock, sucking hard.

"Fuck, woman, so good."

She gently massage his balls as she kept sucking him hard and fast. He couldn't hold back and he filled her mouth with his salty goodness. She looked up at him and swallowed every last drop. He never got tired of seeing that. Now it was her turn.

"Strip. I want to eat that pussy. NOW!"

She tore her clothes off at lightning speed.

"Couch!"

She sat down as she was told. He knelt in front of her and spread her legs wide, burying his face in that sweet pussy. He sucked and licked her so hard her body was quaking hard as she screamed.

"Oh fuck, Dean, so fuckin' good."

"Don't move!"

He stood and she saw that he was rock hard again. He slid into her, thrusting hard and fast.

"Fuck me harder baby."

He increased the power and speed of his thrusts, fucking that hot, wet pussy harder then ever before. Their bodies quickly took flight, like two horny demons flying through the night sky, breathing hard, drenched in sweat as they exploded in orgasms so intense, words escaped them and all they do was moan, and moan loudly. He sat down next to her, barely able to catch his breath.

"Damn, baby, that was so fuckin' hot."

"Oh, Dean," was all she had left in her.

"How about a dip in the pool to cool off?"

"Especially that fire you left between my legs."

'Damn, woman!"

They wrapped themselves in towels and walked out the back door to the pool. After dropping the towels, they climbed in, splashing and playing like teenagers. Dean pulled her close, the warmth of his skin reigniting that fire down below. He felt her hand wrap around his dick and start stroking. He threw his head back and groaned loudly, as she felt his erection grow bigger and harder. He slid a couple of fingers inside heroic causing her to gasp loudly.

"Oh, Dean, I wanna fuck."

"Grass, now!"

She climbed out and laid down in the grass next to the pool. Dean followed, laying on top of her, and sliding his dick inside her. Unlike what they had just done on the couch, his thrusts were slow and sensual. She arched her back, aching to get him even deeper inside her. He took his hands and ran them up her beautiful stomach and wrapped them around her, holding her close. They spent the next several hours passionately making love together. She lost count of how many times her amazing lover sent her into orbit, as her entire body was tinging with electric heat. Both of them exhausted, they collapsed together, gazing up at the bright blue sky. After another quick dip in the pool, they went inside and showered. They both opted for jammies as they planned on a quiet night in. Well, maybe not quiet, depending on how horny they got, but definitely staying in. They went into the kitchen and decided on tacos for dinner. After they ate, Dean they sat on the couch together for a night of movie watching. Holly curled up in a chair and went to sleep.

"I love you."

"Me too, babe."

Dean wrapped an arm around Alex as she laid her head on his shoulder. He again found himself feeling so grateful this amazing woman let him back in her life. He loved her more than he ever knew was possible. He started thinking about the song he'd written, deciding that it would be his wedding gift to her. She had always loved hearing him sing, so he would perform it for her at the wedding. He sighed contentedly and kissed the top of her head. After a couple more movies and their favorite late night talk show, they headed off to bed, quickly falling asleep after their eventful day.

They spent the next couple of days getting things booked for the wedding. Since they were having it at the their farm, they didn't have the worry of finding a place. They hired a local caterer to do the wedding and the rehearsal dinner. Alex decided on a white sun dress, while Dean opted for white pants and white button down shirt. They both decided to wear white cowboy boots, an ode to both Alex's dad, and because they loved farm life so much.

Tracey bought matching sun dresses for her daughters. Alex had her friends each pick their favorite pastel color for their dress. Dean talked to his LA friends and they all agreed, as did Chris to all wear white like Dean. They were sitting in the kitchen completely overwhelmed at how much their friends were helping them. Dean tried to pay for his friends' flights but were having none of it.

"So, who do you have coming in from LA?"

"Lookin' for a new rock star?"

"No way, I snagged my man!"

"I have two members from Dark Horse, Andy York and Damon Jackson. Along with them, my friend Mikael Alfredsson will also be flying in."

"Wow, I'm fans of all of them. Can't wait to meet them!"

"Mikael would be perfect for Hannah. Shame he has a bitchy girlfriend."

"Maybe he'll see Hannah and fall in love with her."

"In a romance novel, maybe."

Laughing, Alex asked, "You read romance novels?"

"Shut up! That's all they had on planes a lot of times."

"Sure, babe, sure."

"Keep that up and the snake doesn't come out to play tonight."

"We'll see about that," she said as she tickled his stomach.

She ducked away just as he was about to tickle her back. He followed her, trying to get her but she kept getting away, both of them laughing hysterically. He finally caught up to her, and started tickling over until she doubled over in laughter. He stopped and pulled her close. She looked up at him as he lowered his mouth down on hers, kissing her hard. She moaned into his mouth as he twirled his tongue with hers. That was all it took to get her dripping wet with desire. She wasn't the only one getting excited as she could feel his dick straining against his pants.

"Bedroom now, my beautiful goddess."

She put an extra sway in her hips as she walked to the bedroom which earned her a loud whistle. He flashed that come hither stare in her direction and her clothes melted right off her body. He removed his jeans and her favorite plaything sprung to life. Fuck, she wanted him inside her. She wagged her finger at him in a come to me gesture, but he stayed put.

"Dean!"

"Baby, you were naughty earlier. Why should I give you what you want?"

"I'll make it worth your while," she said in a smoky, sexy voice.

"Prove it."

"Get on the bed first."

He laid down on the bed. She straddled him and kissed him hard, her tongue eagerly exploring his mouth. Before he could kiss her back, she had moved down to his chest, teasing his nipples with her sexy tongue. She showered his abs with kisses, stopping at his happy trail. She ran her tongue down that sexy line of dark hair until her luscious lips were wrapped around his cock. She bounced her head up and down, sucking hard, running her tongue up and down his massive shaft, stopping to twirl her tongue around the head. She was driving him fucking crazy with desire.

"I need to be inside you."

"Not until I say so."

He groaned with a mix of desire and agony, as he wanted more than anything to feel her hot, wet pussy wrapped around him. She started running her tongue up and down his thighs, with a light sweep across his balls every time she switched legs, until he couldn't take it one more second.

"Fuck, sit on my cock baby."

Flashing him a wicked smile, knowing the effect she was having on him, she got even naughtier. While still straddling him, her body in full view of his gorgeous blue eyes, she started pleasuring herself. She felt him writhing beneath her, desperate to have his dick where her fingers were. He was at the point of begging now.

"Baby, I can't stand another second of not being inside you."

After a little more teasing, she lowered her body onto his, taking every last inch of that massive cock deep inside her body. He was groaning and growling louder than she'd ever heard him, relieved that he could finally feel that hot wet pussy sliding up and down his dick. He would never tire of seeing her, feeling her, loving her, fucking her. He ran his hands up and down her body as she moaned, getting closer and closer to that magical apex they loved reaching together. Their bodies completely in sync, they both exploded together in another in a series of mind blowing orgasms. She collapsed down on his chest as he held her against him.

"My naughty, naughty goddess."

"Mmm, you were incredible."

Chapter Twenty-Three

The weeks leading up to the wedding flew by and all of a sudden, it was the Wednesday before the ceremony. They were going over their checklist when Dean's cell phone rang.

"Hello?"

"Oh hey Chris."

"Hang on let me check."

"Babe, Chris wants to know if we want to meet him and Tracey at the club tonight?"

"Sure, that sounds like fun."

"She said yeah. What time? See ya then."

"Chris said they'll meet us in the parking lot at 6."

"Oh, so we have a couple of hours to kill then."

"Did ya have somethin' in mind?"

She took his hand and led him back to bed. After a couple more hours of setting the sheets on fire, Alex and Dean showered and got ready to head down to the club to meet Chris and Tracey. They got there just as Chris was parking so they parked next to them. The parking lot was pretty full tonight, so Alex was hoping they would be able to get a table or at least find four seats together at the bar. When they walked in, Doug led them to the private rooms at the back of the club. Tracey was behind Alex and Dean so they couldn't see her sending a quick text. Doug opened the door and turned on the light.

"Surprise!"

Alex looked around the room, smiling when she saw the rest of the Dirty Girl club, Hannah, Margie and George, as well as Dean's friends from LA and their wives. There was a huge banner with 'Congratulations Alex and Dean' printed on it as well as a table with some gifts. They made their way around the room greeting everyone. Dean introduced her to Mikael, Andy, and Damon, as well as Andy's wife Lizzie and Damon's wife Amy. Dean finally got to meet the Dirty Girls and their husbands.

"Thanks for surprising me by flying in early. Where's Liza?"

Mikael responded, "She didn't want to spend that much time out here. She'll be here in a couple days."

Dean was about to comment when Chris stood up front and made an announcement that was met with a lot of cheering.

"Ladies, you'll be heading to the room next door for your party, while us dudes party in here."

Tracey took Alex's arm and headed next door, with the rest of the women following them. The room was decorated just for Alex. There was a table with food and drinks and another with tiaras and feather boas for them to put on. They took a ton of fun pictures together and were getting ready to have some food when they heard a knock on their door. As Tracey walked over to answer the door, the rest of the girls moved their chairs to the middle of the room. Margie put a chair for Alex in front of the rest. Once she was seated, Tracey opened the door. Alex's jaw dropped to the floor.

"Howdy, ma'am. I hear you're getting ready to get married. Before you do, your friends wanted to give you one last thrill."

Alex was speechless. Standing before her was one sexy cowboy. He turned on some music and started dancing in front of Alex, as he slowly removed his shirt. Holy shit, he's so damn hot, she thought as she wiped drool off her chin. She could hear the rest of girls yelling, none louder than Debbie, since she had a thing for hot cowboys. He took off his boots and jeans as he moved closer to Alex, placing his hands on her shoulders. It took every ounce of her restraint not to put her hands on that sexy chest.

Putting his hand out, he said, "Dance with me, little lady."

Her face a bright crimson, she stood. The sexy cowboy stood behind her, grinding his hips into her. She started moving with him, her friends cheering even louder, as they snapped a ton of pictures. He sat her back in the chair and danced a few more songs, ending his set with a hotter than hell lap dance. Alex almost fell out of her chair a few times, laughing and cheering along with her friends. She hoped like hell the men couldn't hear anything through the wall!

When he was done, he gave Alex a kiss on the hand and a hug. Debbie also got a hug and she may or may not have pinched his ass! He got dressed and headed out. They girls spent the next couple of hours laughing and talking, as they ate and drank. A little while later, they had another knock on the door, this time Chris telling them to head back over.

While the ladies were having their fun, the guys had just as exciting of a celebration. Like the ladies, they had a knock on their door. Chris opened the door to a woman dressed as a nun. She walked over to where Dean was sitting.

"Your friends invited me here to give you a blessing prior to your wedding."

She turned on some sexy music and started dancing, as she removed her habit. All she had on underneath was pink lace underwear. Her dancing was met with quite a bit of catcalling and whistles. The guys all had their phones out snapping pictures and videos. Once she was done, she headed out after congratulating Dean and posing for a few photos with the guys. Chris headed next door to bring the girls back over.

Once everyone was back in one room, Chris put two chairs up by the gift table so Dean and Alex could open their presents. Of course, all the gifts were pranks, sending them home with a variety of sex toys and naughty lingerie. Once they were done with gifts, Chris popped a couple bottles of champagne open and poured everyone a glass. Everyone was standing with their glasses raised as Chris toasted Dean and Alex.

"Dean, we've been friends since Kindergarten and it has been one hell of a ride. I've seen you go through more ups and downs than anyone should have to and you managed to come out on top. Returning home and reuniting with the love of your life has done wonders for you. I've never seen you so happy. I love you like a brother. Alex, though I've known you a much shorter amount of time, I love you just as much. It's clear the two of you were put on this earth to be together. I wish you both all the love and happiness in the world for the rest of your days on earth. To Dean and Alex!"

In unison, everyone else echoed Chris, "To Dean and Alex!"

Chris turned on some music so everyone could dance. Everyone there had a significant other except for Mikael and Hannah. He walked over to her and sat down.

"Hannah, right?"

"Y-y-y-ou remembered my name?"

"Of course."

"But you're a famous rock star."

"Yep. And this rock star would like the honor of a dance."

"Ummm, are you sure?"

"Yeah."

Hannah stood and followed him to the dance floor. Mikael took her into his arms and he felt a spark like nothing he felt with his current girl-friend, Liza. He had to quickly put that out of his head. Liza would be here a couple of days before the wedding. He was having a hard time though. There was definitely something intriguing about her. She was unlike the women he was used to being around, and honestly, that made him like her even more.

Once the club was getting ready to close, they all started to file out. Doug brought in a couple of bags so they could pack up their gifts. Alex couldn't wait to try out some of their new goodies. They put the bags in the back of Dean's truck. They hugged everyone goodbye and told them they'd see them on Saturday, then headed home. They carried their bags inside and Dean noticed Alex had a naughty look on her face.

"I can only imagine what you're thinkin'."

"Just clean thoughts here."

"Liar!"

Alex feigned shock, pouting and putting her hands on her hips.

"I'm an angel."

"I bet I can prove otherwise!"

"I dare you to try!"

Dean scooped her up in his arms and carried her to their bedroom, putting her down on the bed. He laid next to her and slid his hands under her shirt, quickly removing it along with her bra. She tried to cover up her breasts with her arms.

"No, no, baby. Leave those sexy breasts out."

He lowered his head and started sucking on them, teasing her hard nipples with his tongue.

"Mmm, so good."

She removed his shirt, marveling as always at the sight of that sexy muscular chest. She wrapped her arms around him and pulled him down, loving the feeling of his chest on hers. He kissed her hard, leaving her no doubt of his desire for her. She reached down and opened his jeans, sliding her hand inside and stroking his cock. His dick responded immediately and he was harder than steel. She started tracing all the veins with her fingers as he groaned loudly.

"God, I wanna fuck."

"Please, my sexy rock star, give it to me hard."

Dean stripped the rest of her clothes off and slid a couple of fingers inside her.

"So fuckin' wet, babe."

"I want you so damn bad."

Dean slid his dick inside her, thrusting hard and fast. He felt her nails raking his back, like the tigress she was. Fuck he loved this woman, this amazing woman who in just a few short days would be his wife. Just the thought of that increased his excitement, and he started pounding her harder and harder as she screamed in ecstasy. He was such an incredible lover that he could send her into orbit no matter what position he fucked her in. He quickly shot his load inside her and moved next to her, chest heaving, body slick with sweat.

"So fuckin' hot, woman!"

"I love you, Dean."

"Love you, babe."

"I think we need to bring our new goodies on our honeymoon."

"Love the way you think!"

About a minute later, Dean was sound asleep, so she pulled the covers up and turned out the light. She laid against him, feeling his hot, naked skin on hers and quickly joined him in dreamland.

The next morning, around mid-morning, they were down by the pond with Holly when they heard a vehicle pulling into their driveway. They headed up just as Mikael, Andy and Damon were getting out a van, along with Amy and Lizzie.

"Farm life definitely agrees with you," Andy said. "Never seen you happier."

Nodding at Alex, Dean replied, "It's all thanks to her.

The other guys started giving Dean shit about being a country boy now. They started heading down toward the pond to talk more, getting Dean caught up on what's been happening in LA and with their bands. Alex noticed Mikael seemed quiet compared to the other guys, like something was bothering him. She didn't really know him, though, so maybe he was always like that.

"We'd love to see the house," Lizzie said with a warm smile.

"Sure, come on in."

Lizzie took Holly inside while she showed Amy and Lizzie around. Suddenly, she remembered why Lizzie looked so familiar to her.

"Lizzie, I kept thinking you looked familiar and now I remember. You're Lizzie Gardner, right?"

"I was until I married that sexy axeman!"

"I read 'Rock World' religiously. I especially love the naughty fantasies you write."

"Thank you. I owe everything to that magazine. I would never have met Andy otherwise."

Lizzie told Alex the story of how she and Andy came to meet.

"Wow, that sounds just like something out of a romance novel."

The three of them sat down at Alex's kitchen table. Even though they'd just met, it felt like they'd been friends for years. She loved hearing Lizzie and Amy's stories about what it like being out in LA with the band and dealing with all the groupies and crazies. All part of the business, but definitely not their favorite part. By the time the guys came inside, the three of them were laughing so hard, they had tears pouring down their cheeks.

Pretending to be worried, Andy asked, "I'm guessing we don't want to know what you three have been up to."

"Girl talk," Lizzie responded.

Alex saw Andy smile at her and it was obvious how much they loved each other. Suddenly realizing she was being a terrible host, Alex asked if she could get anyone something to drink or some lunch.

"Actually, babe, the guys were just saying they'd love it if we'd show them some of the sights. How about we start at our favorite diner for lunch then take them on a tour?"

"Sounds great."

Since there was room for all of them, they decided to take the rental van, with Dean driving and Alex next to him since they knew where they were going. They headed over to the diner and enjoyed lunch together then headed out for their tour. They spent the next few hours driving through most of their little town, definitely a huge difference from LA, from what Alex could gather, having never been there herself. She found herself starting to get a little worried that Dean might realize he missed that scene and want to head back, but she had to push that thought out of her head for now. When they were done, Dean drove back to the house. After everyone said their goodbyes, his friends headed back to their hotel.

Alex sat down on the porch, and Dean joined her.

"You miss LA, don't you?"

"Not at all."

"I thought hearing them talk about the scene would make you realize it you wanted to go back."

"Actually, the opposite. I was miserable out there. This is where I belong."

"I'm so glad. I couldn't have handled losing you again."

"Never."

"I was wondering something else."

"What?"

"Is Mikael always that sullen and quiet?"

"No, he's usually the comic of the group."

"I wonder if it's because his girlfriend didn't come with him."

"No clue."

Dean didn't seem like he wanted to stay on that subject so Alex let it drop. Deciding to change the subject, she looked over at her hot man.

"How about a horseback ride?"

"Wouldn't you rather ride me?"

She gave him a playful swat on his sexy ass.

"That'll be later, my sexy cowboy."

Now it was her turn for a swat on the ass. They headed out to the stables and did a few laps around the farm. The sun was just starting it's descent, but they still had plenty of light left. As they rode, the sun slowly lowered making their ride even more romantic. They stopped at the dock and dismounted, tying the horses to the two hitching posts Alex had there. They sat down on the dock, gazing at the sky. Dean put his arm around her, as she laid her head on his shoulder.

"Baby, I can't believe in just two short days, we'll be married. I love you."

"Oh Dean, I love you so much."

Dean put a hand under her chin and gently lifted her head, kissing her tenderly. Unlike the way he usually kissed her, his tongue slid into her mouth with a gentleness, as she swirled her tongue around his. They spent a deliciously long time locked in their passionate embrace, as they kissed with increasing passion, his tongue getting more eager inside her mouth.

"Baby, let's head back. I really want to take you to bed and make love."

"Oh, Dean."

They got back on their horses and once they had them secured in the stable, they headed right for their bedroom, and spent the next several hours making passionate and tender love together, until they drifted off into a blissful night's sleep.

Chapter Twenty-Four

Dean woke up first, his stomach growling after their night of passion. He put his arms around Alex, causing her to stir and slowly wake up. He leaned in for a kiss as he rubbed her sexy ass.

"HUngry?" he asked

"Yeah, starving from that incredible lovin' you gave me last night."

They were still naked from their hot steamy night together, so they put on robes and wen to the kitchen. Alex grabbed her griddle and made French toast for them, while Dean got the coffee brewing. After they finished breakfast, Alex cleaned up and got everything put away, since people would be in the house later.

She sat in his lap and asked, "Is it really the day before our wedding?"

"Yeah, baby."

"I can't wait for the rehearsal dinner tonight."

"Me either. Wanna sneak over to the studio?"

"What'd you have in mind?"

"You'll see."

"Mmmm, Dean."

They didn't even bother getting dressed, each just throwing on a pair of sneakers. Dean grabbed the bags from the party the other night.

They sped over to the studio and right into the oasis Dean built for them.

"What're you gonna do to me?" Alex asked.

"Anything your heart desires."

"Or anything my body desires."

"Of course."

"Then get your clothes off. Now!"

Slowly and teasingly, he exposed his sexy body as she stood there gawking. Fuck, he gets me hot, she thought to herself. Licking her lips, dying to wrap them around his cock, she got impatient and ripped the rest of his clothes off.

"Now, let me see you stroke that cock."

He gazed up at her as he took his dick into his hand, slowly stroking it. She was so turned on, her knees got weak. He moaned as he kept stroking himself. Unable to wait another second, she walked over, got on her knees and wrapped her sexy mouth around his dick, sucking and licking hard. Dean threw his head back and groaned as his hot lover sucked off his rock hard erection. When she couldn't stand not having him inside her any longer, she stood and quickly got naked herself then returned to the couch.

She lowered herself onto Dean's lap, taking his dick inside her. She was so wet, he slid in easily. Pressing her incredible breasts against his sexy chest, she fucked him hard and fast until the both exploded. She loved the feeling of his dick inside her more than anything else she'd ever felt and couldn't get enough of being naked with her sexy man.

"So fuckin' good, but my turn now."

He looked through the bags until he found the box he was looking for.

"Get that hot little ass in bed."

After she laid down, Dean put the blindfold on her and tied her wrists to the headboard with silk scarves. She was so turned on, she could barely contain herself. She loved giving him total control over her body.

"Spread those sexy legs and show me that sweet pussy."

She opened her legs and the feeling of being on display got her even hotter. A loud moan escaped her lips, her pussy throbbing with desire as she writhed on the bed, aching to be touched.

"Touch that sweet pussy for me," he commanded.

Alex took a deep breath, and started teasing her own pussy. She moaned with pleasure as she got herself off. She couldn't see her lover, but she knew she was getting him hot when she heard him moaning. She started imagining it was him touching her and she harder, moaning louder as she got closer to that sweet explosion she loved so much.

"So fuckin' sexy," he growled.

She moaned even louder when she felt his sexy cock slide inside her slick, wet pussy. She grabbed his ass, pushing him in harder and deeper as he fucked her. After watching her pleasure herself, he was close to the edge and quickly filled her pussy with his cum, before he could bring her to orgasm.

"Wow, you must have really liked the show I gave you."

"I wanna see your hot naked body on the desk now!"

He freed her wrists but he made her keep the blindfold on. He walked her over to the desk and helped her sit. Not knowing where he was, when he would touch her was exciting her even more. Suddenly, she felt Dean spread her legs wide and jam his tongue eagerly into her sweet pussy, licking and sucking until her entire body shook with pleasure. She threw her head back and screamed. Instead of stopping, Dean kept licking and sucking her clit as he slid a couple fingers inside her. He brought her to orgasm after orgasm, each one more intense than the one before it until she was screaming at the top of her lungs.

"Oh god, oh Dean, I can't take it anymore, oh fuck, please, holy shit."

His tongue kept up its assault between her legs, as her body quivered harder and harder. The pleasure was more intense than anything she'd ever felt. Her entire body was on fire and she completely forgot where she was, even who she with how incredible he was making her feel. Watching her enjoy this so much gave him another hard-on. He slowly entered her pussy, groaning loudly.

"Baby, tell me how that feels."

"Your cock feels so damn good inside me. I love when you fuck me."

Each stroke left her feeling like she was floating. Her pussy was on fire and she felt like she was close to squirting like she did the other day. She lifted her hips trying to get the angle she needed to have Dean's dick hit her g-spot. After a few more slow but powerful thrusts, she felt her dam burst, soaking Dean's dick with her love juice. Her incredible orgasm sent him over the edge and he filled her with his salty delicious cream.

"Fuck, woman, that was incredible."

"Mmm, yes it was."

"I guess we oughta get back to the house."

"Okay, but could we do one little thing first?"

"What?"

"A nice soak in that amazing tub?"

"Ready when you are, babe."

Dean lowered the lights before they got in the tub. The warm water and massage jets left them both feeling relaxed and re-energized. They got dried off then put their robes and sneakers back on to head home. They had just parked when they heard a car coming up the driveway. They turned and saw the rental van.

"Shit. We're never gonna get inside before they see us."

Alex was too mortified to respond. She just sat in the truck, her face turning a bright crimson.

"Fuck it," Dean said as he got out of the truck.

Alex heard his friends laughing when they saw him. She couldn't help but start laughing herself. She got to join him. They were giving Dean all kinds of shit when she walked over. Suddenly feeling bold, what came out of her mouth quickly shut them up.

"Laugh all you want, but think about this. He just spent the last hour fucking my brains out."

Before anyone could respond, she turned and walked into the house, missing the look of pride on Dean's face. She looked out the front door in time to see them all bowing to him as if he was a king. After a few more minutes they all came inside. Dean walked over and whispered in Alex's ear.

"You're the best."

Turning to his friends, Dean said, "Make yourselves at home. We just need to grab a quick shower and get dressed."

Mikael responded, "I don't wanna hear any fucking in there."

Everyone laughed. Alex was happy to hear him joking, seeming more like the person Dean had described. They grabbed a quick shower together then got dressed and rejoined the group. She started feeling bad that Dean hadn't had much a chance to spend time with his friends.

"Dean, why don't you head out with your friends. I can get everything set up for tonight."

Before he could respond, Andy spoke up, "No way. We came over today to help."

Alex smiled and thanked the group for giving their time up this way. They all headed out back so Alex could show them where they were planning on putting everything. Once she was done, handing out assignments, finishing up in under an hour. All that was left now was everyone getting cleaned up and changed. Dean took the guys over to his house, while the girls stayed at Alex's. Amy was getting her shower, so Lizzie and Alex were in the kitchen talking. They looked outside when they heard another car in the driveway and saw a cab.

"That must be Liza," Lizzie said as she rolled her eyes.

"Not a fan?"

"Not really. I don't like the way she treats Mikael. Fair warning, she can be a bit of a 'mean girl.' Try not to let her get to you."

"Thanks."

Alex was about to ask Lizzie something else when she heard a very snotty hello outside her door. Putting on her sweetest smile, she walked over and opened the door.

"Hello, Liza and welcome to my home. I'm…"

"Whatever," she said as she strolled in on her way-to-high stilettos.

"Can I get you something to drink?"

"Water."

"Coming right up."

Alex grabbed a glass, put some ice in and start filling it with tap water.

"Mineral water, not that shit."

"I apologize, but I don't have mineral water."

"Well, what good are you then? And where the hell is Mikael?"

"Dean took the guys over to his house to get cleaned up before the rehearsal dinner."

"Oh, yeah, that," she said with a bored yawn.

Alex quietly walked outside and sat down on her porch. Lizzie followed her.

"I'm sorry about her."

"Don't be."

"I promise we won't let her spoil your day."

"Thanks."

A few minutes later, Amy walked outside and sighed heavily.

"You're turn, Lizzie."

"Thanks."

Amy sat down with Alex.

"I couldn't sit in there with her," Amy whispered.

"Exactly why Lizzie and I were out here."

Once Lizzie was ready, she joined Amy and Alex. Alex got up to go get her shower and get dressed. While she was in there, the guys got back. Lizzie let Mikael know Liza was inside. Once he went in, Lizzie told them what happened with Alex. She looked at Dean and smiled.

"Your fiancée is amazing. She handled the way Liza treated her very well."

"She sure is. If you'll excuse me, I need to make sure she doesn't need help in the shower."

Dean headed inside, stopped to greet Liza then headed into the bathroom.

"Hey, baby, came to see if you needed a hand."

Alex smiled and responded, "I'd rather have your dick."

"Later, babe."

She finished up in the shower and stepped out. Dean wrapped her in a towel and held her tight.

"Just think, this time tomorrow, you'll be Mrs. Alexandra Fox."

"I know baby, and I can't wait. I love you."

"I love you."

She opened the bathroom door to head to the bedroom when she heard Liza and Mikael arguing about staying for the dinner tonight and coming to the wedding tomorrow She could see how upset Mikael was.

They quietly walked to the bedroom and shut the door. After Alex finished getting dressed, they headed back to the living room. The rest of their guests would be arriving shortly, so they walked outside. About half an hour later, the caterer arrived, so Alex showed them where to set up. A little while later, everyone was here, so they all headed out back to the tables and sat down. Dean stood up in front of the tables and Alex joined him.

"Thank you so much for coming to celebrate with us the night before I marry the woman of my dreams. Tonight is all about fun, love, and celebrating, so please go help yourself to some food."

Everyone insisted Alex and Dean go through the line first. After they got their food and sat down, they noticed Mikael and Liza still seated. Alex walked over to them.

"Feel free to get in line."

"I expected to be served," Liza responded.

"I apologize. I'd be happy to get you both a plate," Alex said with a warm smile.

"That's the least you can do since I'm stuck at this ridiculous party."

Hannah had just gotten back with her food and heard the way Liza spoke to her friend. She walked over and Alex saw Mikael's face light up.

"Alex, go enjoy dinner with you sexy husband-to-be. I'm happy to get them each a plate," Hannah said.

"Thank you, Hannah."

As Alex went back to sit with Dean, Hannah asked them each what they wanted then headed up. Mikael got up and went with her, causing Dean and Alex to exchange raised eyebrows. Once everyone had their food, they sat and ate, laughing and talking. Everyone except Liza, that is. She sat there looking like she was smelling a fart. After everyone had finished eating, Alex turned on some music and pointed the group to the dance floor they rented.

Since Liza wouldn't lower herself to dance with the rest of the group, Mikael danced with Hannah. Alex swore he looked ten times happier when he was with Hannah as opposed to his snotty girlfriend, and she seemed to be into him as well. The party lasted until close to midnight,as nobody wanted to stop dancing. Dean was getting tired, as was Alex, so he addressed the group one last time.

"Thank you all so much for spending tonight with us. We love you and we can't wait to see you all back there tomorrow for the wedding."

Everyone filtered through, hugging Dean and Alex, telling them how excited they were for tomorrow. When Mikael and Liza came through, he hugged them both but Liza could only manage an eye roll. Alex again noticed Mikael's eyes on Hannah. If only he could dump that asshole, he would be perfect or Hannah, Alex thought to herself. Chris and Tracey were the last ones to leave. They helped clean up then headed home themselves.

Dean and Alex went to bed shortly after everyone was gone. They were too exhausted to even make love but there would be plenty of time for that on their honeymoon. Dean pulled her close, kissing her tenderly on her beautiful lips.

"Baby, I can't believe the day is finally here. I love you."

"I'm so happy. I love you too."

Dean turned off the light and they both quickly fell into a deep sleep, holding each other tight.

Chapter Twenty-Five

They awakened early the morning of their wedding. After a quick breakfast, they went over to the studio for a soak in the tub before they started getting ready. When they got to the studio, Dean took her into the office and handed her a big box with a red bow on it.

"What's this?"

"Open it, silly."

She opened the box and her eyes went wide. Inside was a beautiful new guitar with her initials engraved on the neck. It was by far the most beautiful guitar she'd ever seen up close.

"This is so beautiful. Thank you so much."

"I can't wait to hear you play it."

"I hope I don't break it with my horrible playing."

"Stop that!"

Alex played a little bit as Dean sat there smiling. He loved how good she sounded. He was impressed that she had never taken a lesson, instead having natural talent. He had been thinking about recording an album and he couldn't think of anyone better to play guitar for him then his bride.

"Baby, when we get back from our honeymoon, I really want to record an album. It's something completely different than anything I did with The Hounds and I just really feel it's important for me to do this."

"I can't wait to hear it."

"Of course, I will need someone to play guitar for me," he said, nodding at her new guitar.

"Me? I would never be good enough."

"I promise you, you're more than good enough. You're amazing. Now, let's take that soak."

As they were sitting there relaxing, Dean felt Alex's soft fingers running down his thigh. He could feel his dick starting to stir. Fuck the loved this woman. She moved closer to him and whispered in his ear.

"Please take me to bed and have your way with me, my sexy king."

That was all it took and boom, his dick was hard as a rock.

"Bed. Now!"

Alex got out of the tub, dried off and walked over to the bed, laying down. She waited not-so-patiently for her lover to join her. Dean got out, dried off and drained the tub then joined his sexy woman in bed. He never got a chance to make a move before Alex was on all fours, her mouth sliding up and down his cock. Damn, she knew how to suck. He reached down and stroked her clit as she kept sucking him, the pressure building quickly. Without a word, she mounted him and took his dick deep inside, fucking him hard and fast until they exploded in ecstasy.

"We better get you back to the house before anyone arrives," Dean said breathlessly.

Dean dropped Alex at her house, then headed back to his farm, as the men would be getting ready there, while the girls would be getting ready at Alex's house. They kissed goodbye, excited that the next time they would see each would be when Alex was walking down the aisle. Alex's friends arrived a little while later and starting helping her get ready. Heather styled her hair while Jan did her makeup. When they were done, Alex couldn't believe the woman she saw looking back at her in the mirror. She went to her bedroom to get dressed. Alex had chosen a simple, flowing white dress and white cowboy boots, along with a simple veil. When she returned to where her friends for waiting, now in their bridesmaids dressed, their jaws dropped.

"You are absolutely stunning," Debbie said.

Dee added, "Dean is going to pass out when he sees you."

"I can't thank you enough for helping me get ready. I had no idea what to do with my hair and I've never worn makeup. I also want to thank you all for being my co-matrons of honor. I have a little something for each of you."

Alex handed them each a small box. They couldn't believe their eyes. Each box contained a pair of one-carat diamond earrings. They each thanked her and put the earrings on, then headed outside to get ready to make their entrance. The photographer took a few pictures of them then got them lined up to walk in. George put his arm out for Alex, a look of pride on his face.

There was a tent setup so that Dean couldn't see Alex until she began her procession. Dean waited up front, dressed in a white western style suit and white cowboy boots. Standing behind him were Chris, Andy, Damon, and Mikael, all dressed in black western style suits and black cowboy boots, with ties matching the dress color of the bridesmaid they would walk with. They were doing their best to keep Dean calm, letting him know how amazing marriage was. Once the men were lined up and ready, the judge nodded to the photographer, and she had them start walking the aisle. Chris's daughters went first, laying white rose petals along the aisle, followed by Debbie, Jan, Heather, and Dee. Once the women were all lined up, the DJ started playing the wedding march. The photographer walked out first so she could take a photo of Alex and George.

George opened the tent and they started their walk down the aisle. Alex kept her eyes on Dean the whole time, smiling at the way his jaw dropped when he saw her. He couldn't believe this woman could get any more beautiful. When she reached the front, George gave her a kiss on the cheek and placed her hand into Dean's. After exchanging vows and rings, the judge handed Dean his microphone, and Chris handed him his guitar.

"Baby, I've been working for weeks on a song to perform for you today. I hope you like it."

After Dean finished singing the most beautiful song Alex had ever heard, the judge pronounced them husband and wife. They kissed passionately. As they turned to walk down the aisle together, the judge made an announcement that resulted in the loudest cheers they'd ever heard.

"Ladies and Gentlemen, it gives me great pleasure to introduce for the first time, Mr, and Mrs. Dean Fox."

Alex and Dean walked down the aisle, followed by Dee & Chris, Heather & Andy, Jan & Damon, and finally, Debbie & Mikael. Once the wedding party had finished their walk, the rest of the guests followed them to the reception area. The photographer took the wedding party along with George and Margie for photos, while the catering staff circulated with appetizers. Once the photos were done, they joined the rest of their guests and sat down so dinner could be served. After dinner, Dean and Alex cut their cake, completely covering each other's faces.

While they got cleaned up, the DJ urged everyone to the dance floor. Like the rehearsal dinner, the night before, Liza couldn't be bothered, so Mikael ended up dancing the night away with Hannah. The party lasted until the wee hours of the morning. Alex and Dean thanked everyone for coming and for their help with everything as they were leaving. Chris and Tracey took Holly with them since the newlyweds would be getting an early start, as they were driving to North Carolina. Dean's LA friends were the last ones to leave. They all hugged goodbye, as they would be heading back to California in the morning,

After the last of the guests had left and the catering staff had finished cleaning up, Dean and Alex headed inside. Dean opened the door, scooped Alex up in his arms, and carried her inside. He put her down then closed and locked the door, and they headed straight to their bedroom.

"Alexandra, my angel, my wife, I love you so much."

"Oh Dean, my sexy, incredible husband, I love you."

"Baby, all I want to do now is get in bed and, for the first time in my life, make love to my wife."

Dean helped her remove her dress and boots then removed his own clothes. Once they were naked, they laid down together and held each other close, more in love than ever. He gently rolled his beautiful wife onto her back and moved on top of her, slowly sliding inside her. They held each other and kissed tenderly while they made love. It was different this time, so much more tender, more loving than ever before.

They became one more than any other time, heart, mind, body, and soul, and now also marriage. They continued loving each other as their bodies slowly began to ascend like two hawks preparing for flight until they were soaring through the night sky, both of the moaning in pure ecstasy. Once they returned to earth, Dean pulled her in close and kissed her tenderly.

"I love you, my beautiful, incredible wife."

"I love you too, my sexy, amazing husband."

"We should probably get some sleep as we have an early start tomorrow."

"Okay, baby. I can't wait. I love North Carolina."

"I promise you baby, you will never forget this trip."

The next morning, they loaded their luggage in Dean's truck and hit the highway. They arrived in North Carolina mid-afternoon. After carrying their luggage into their rental house, they enjoyed a romantic dinner and a walk on the beach. They stopped and laid down in the sand for a little while, holding and kissing each other passionately, then retired to their bedroom, both of them boiling over with desire.

After removing each other's clothes, they laid down in bed together and made love in a variety of positions, experiencing wave after wave of passionate, intense pleasure until the morning light streamed in through their windows. They got up, dressed, and took another long walk on the beach before they returned to their room and napped until dinnertime. They did a little bit of sightseeing around the town where they were staying, but the majority of their time they spent naked in bed, where they got plenty of use out of the naughty gifts from their bachelor/bachelorette party. On their last night in North Carolina, they snuck down to the beach after dark and made love in the sand. Their honeymoon flew by way to quickly and before they knew it, their truck was back in their driveway. They headed home, their home, and immediately went to the their bedroom.

As they had done so many times before, Alex and Dean eagerly undressed and got in bed together. They spent the next several hours in bed passionately touching, tasting, kissing, and fucking each other until they were both completely spent. Their chests heaving, bodies drenched in sweat and tingling with intense pleasure, they drifted off to sleep, lost in the ecstasy of wedded bliss.

They spent the next several months in their recording studio making the album Dean had always envisioned. Unlike the cookie cutter music they were forced to record as part of their contract, Dean had the freedom to do what he wanted on this one. The songs were more emotional, more honest, and more true to who he was. Alex was easily able to learn all songs and played guitar on the album. To round out the players, Dean visited the local high school and auditioned a bassist and drummer. The album sounded great and was quickly picked up by an up-and-coming label. Having a big name like Dean on their label was a huge win for them.

To help promote the album, they did a small tour through the northeast, and were met with sold out crowds for every show. Alex loved that they could tour together, and especially that they could bring Holly with them. Once they had completed the tour, Dean was unsure what he wanted to do next. One night, as they were eating dinner, he looked like he had something on his mind.

"What'cha thinkin' about, my sexy man?"

"I finally know what I want to do next."

"Do tell!"

'I enrolled in Penn State's online degree program. I want to get my teaching degree, so I can help keep music alive in our school."

She got up and hugged him. "I know you're going to be amazing. How about we go celebrate?"

"What'd you have in mind."

She kissed him hard, caressing his tongue with hers. She headed to their bedroom with Dean right behind her.

"Stand right here," she commanded.

She lifted his shirt off, running her soft hands all over his chest and back, driving him wild. He started to lift her shirt, but she stopped him.

"I'm in charge tonight," she said sternly.

She opened and removed his pants, loving that he was going

commando. His already hard dick spilled out, just begging for her lips. But he would have to wait.

"Bed! Now!"

Dean laid down, a huge smile on his face, eager to see what his naughty goddess of a wife had in store for him. Standing far enough away that he couldn't touch her, she did a slow strip tease for him. With each piece of her clothing she removed, she ran her hands over her own body, and she could see she was having exactly the effect she wanted. He was writhing on the bed, aching to touch her, and even more, to be touched by her. She opened the drawer where they kept all their toys and grabbed the blindfold and silk scarves. His breathing became more shallow as she tied him up and blindfolded him.

She was careful to be quiet so he had no idea where she was.

"Baby, you're driving me wild."

"Quiet! You may only speak when I tell you to."

He suddenly felt her hands running up his legs, purposely ignoring his cock. She ran her tongue along the insides of his thighs, as her lips sucked hard. He badly wanted to groan, but he knew he had to keep quiet. He felt her climb onto the bed and straddle him. She started running her tongue all over his chest and stomach, her ass touching his dick just lightly enough that he thought he would explode.

"You may speak. Tell me what you want and it better be dirty or I'm getting dressed."

"Please, I wanna feel your hot mouth wrapped around my cock, sucking me hard."

He felt her soft body slide down his, causing him to quiver from head to toe. She wrapped her soft lips around his erection, as she dragged her tongue along his shaft.

"Fuck, woman, you're incredible."

"Where do you want to come, baby?"

Your sexy mouth."

She sucked him harder and faster, gently squeezing his balls under he shot a huge load of his delicious salty cream in her mouth. She removed the blindfold so he could watch her swallow every last drop, as she licked her lips. That was all it took and he was hard again.

"I'm going to untie you now, but remember, I'm still in charge."

"Mmmm, okay, babe."

Alex untied him, then laid down on the bed next to him, spreading her legs wide.

"Get that tongue in my pussy. NOW!"

He loved tasting her, so he quickly moved on top of her, his head between her sexy thighs. He licked her pussy hard, sucking on her clit as she writhed and screamed in ecstasy.

"Fuck, that feels so good. I wanna feel your fingers inside me while you keep sucking my clit."

He took his fingers and stroked her g-spot hard while he kept sucking her clit. She screamed louder and louder as he entire body was bucking off the bed until he felt his fingers get drenched by her sweet juices. He took his tongue and lapped up all her sweet honey. She was so sensitive after her intense orgasm, his tongue was driving her wild.

"I see your cock is hard again. I think you better get that inside me. Get up here and fuck my pussy!"

He emitted a low growl as he jammed his cock inside her pussy, still slick from her orgasm. Fuck, she felt so good wrapped around him.

"Oh god, fuck me harder. So fuckin' good."

He pounded her harder than ever before, his balls slapping her ass hard. They were so in love, so hot for each other, their bodies, hearts, and souls in sync, as they simultaneously rode wave after wave of the most intense pleasure they'd felt yet. She loved feeling his hot cream deep inside her. They were both drenched in sweat and other delicious fluids, as they laid there catching their breath. They took a quick shower together then headed to bed, both of them exhausted.

After a long night of much-needed sleep, they finished breakfast then decided to head down to the park for a walk. They were about halfway around the park when they heard a couple of familiar voices. They stopped and looked at each other, both clearly puzzled, as they overheard a heated conversation.

"Why the fuck did you make me come back here," Liza angrily shouted.

"I saw how much leaving LA helped Dean and I wanted that too," Mikael responded.

'Well, this sucks."

"Just give it time, you'll learn to like it."

"Whatever."

Dean and Alex went a differently way back to their truck, so they didn't embarrass Mikael and headed home.

"I can't wait to hear that story," Dean said as they rode home, thankful they had found their happily ever after.

About the Author

Samantha Michaels was born in 1973 in the small town of Abington, PA and was raised and still lives in Hatboro, PA (both suburbs of Philadelphia). She is married to her high school sweetheart and they have a rescue dog, a beautiful Black Lab named Holly.

When she's not writing or working at her full-time job, she enjoys watching her Philly sports team (hopefully) win, listening to heavy metal/hard rock music, Texas Hold Em, reading, and spending time with friends and family.

Her love of reading began at a young age, thanks to her mother and Sesame Street. Her mom read to her constantly, and by three years old, she was reading on her own, and hasn't stopped. This eventually turned into a love of writing. She was writing for herself and then for a small group of friends, one of whom told her she should be writing books. She took her friends advice and has since published several romance books with plenty more on the way.

For updates and a free book, click **here** to sign up for my newsletter.

Also by
Samantha Michaels

Leather and Lace

www.ingramcontent.com/pod-product-compliance
Lightning Source LLC
Chambersburg PA
CBHW020634180626
46816CB00003B/953